"I love you like this . . ."

"Warm, wanton ....
Adam added a.................
across Kara's br............ever met a
woman who can make me lose control the
way you do."

"I like the idea of making you lose control,"
she murmured silkily, enraptured by his
touch. She slowly trailed a finger up his
thigh.

Adam closed his eyes, and desire returned
with an intensity he would have thought
impossible, considering the force of their
earlier lovemaking. "I think," he said, "that
you're making me crazy again."

Kara's answering laughter was light and
breathless as she moved beneath him. "Let's
be crazy together."

JoAnn Ross , one of Temptation's most productive authors, once entertained the idea of dropping out and becoming a beachcomber in Hawaii. Though she's too energetic a person to settle for such a placid existence, JoAnn was delighted to explore her island fantasy through vivacious Kara Tiernan, the heroine of *Worth Waiting For*. All daydreams aside, JoAnn is supremely contented with real life in Phoenix with her husband.

Books by JoAnn Ross

HARLEQUIN TEMPTATION

HARLEQUIN INTRIGUE

Don't miss any of our special offers. Write to us at the following address for information on our newest releases.

Harlequin Reader Service
901 Fuhrmann Blvd., P.O. Box 1397, Buffalo, NY 14240
Canadian address: P.O. Box 603,
Fort Erie, Ont. L2A 5X3

Published January 1988

ISBN 0-373-25287-0

Worth Waiting For

JoANN ROSS

Harlequin Books

TORONTO • NEW YORK • LONDON
AMSTERDAM • PARIS • SYDNEY • HAMBURG
STOCKHOLM • ATHENS • TOKYO • MILAN

1

EVEN FROM THIS DISTANCE, Kara Tiernan recognized him immediately. He had, unsurprisingly, grown older—lines fanned out from his eyes and there was a sprinkling of silver in the golden strands of his hair. She wondered if his devastating smile had diminished in wattage. Not that she was at all interested; she'd gotten her fill of that smile years ago.

At the moment, however, the individual trudging through the sparkling coral sand was definitely not at his charismatic best. He had discarded his gray suit jacket and tie and rolled his starched white sleeves up to the elbow, but it was obvious that the lightweight wool slacks were far more suitable to northern California weather than the tropical Hawaiian sun. And his shoes—black wingtips, for heaven's sake, Kara thought critically—were definitely not proper beach footwear.

Despite his alien attire, the quantity of luggage he carried suggested that the man was planning to stay for some time. Since the only two residences on this stretch of isolated beach were her own cottage and this one, Kara put down her hammer with a resigned sigh and waited.

Adam Lassiter was not filled with what is called in the islands the aloha spirit. He was hot, thirsty, tired and cursing his decision to come to Kauai, the most remote of the inhabited islands making up the Hawaiian chain.

Back in San Francisco, he'd thought the idea made sense—a quiet, restful place to escape to, if only for a few days, from the grueling demands of his work. But now, as his shoes filled with sand and he melted under the tropical sun, Adam was wondering if he had only fallen under the spell of Colin Tiernan's superb narrative skills.

"A paradise," Colin had assured him expansively over fried calamari and pasta at San Francisco's popular Washington Square Bar and Grill. While the other diners, conservatively and properly clad in three-piece pin-striped suits, negotiated high-flying deals over their power lunches, the denim-clad novelist had proceeded to describe a heaven on earth: rich in foliage, rimmed by sparkling beaches, surrounded by pristine ocean waters and home to the most beautiful women found anywhere on earth.

Thus far, the only foliage Adam had been given an opportunity to see was the tall, tasseled sugarcane flanking the road the driver had turned onto soon after leaving Lihue Airport. After what had seemed an eternity of tearing along in a cloud of red dust, with the man apparently trying to hit every pothole in the dirt road, he'd come to a sudden stop with a screech of brakes and the information that this was as far as the road went. From now on, Adam was on his own.

The driver had, Adam admitted reluctantly, offered to help carry his many bags to their final destination. But unused to such comradeship from a taxi driver, and vaguely embarrassed by the stranger's exuberant friendliness, Adam had declined.

That had been twenty long, hot minutes ago, and Adam had made the decision that if he didn't reach Colin's house within the next thirty seconds, he was going to throw himself, fully clothed, into the Pacific Ocean. Then, once he had cooled off, he was going to trudge back up that damned haul cane road, flag down the first car he saw, request a ride to the airport and catch a plane back to San Francisco.

It was then that he saw her. At first Adam wondered if she might be nothing but a mirage, the product of a heat-crazed mind. She was clad in a brilliantly flowered bikini top and faded cutoff jeans, her skin tanned to a warm, dark honey. Clouds of thick, unruly hair caressed her shoulders in sunlit strands of glistening copper, gold and bronze. If she had been perched on a rock jutting out of the water, instead of sitting atop the roof of the small, vine-covered house, Adam could have easily believed that he had stumbled upon a mythical siren.

He was unaware of straightening his spine and squaring his shoulders as he continued toward her, but from her vantage point above him, Kara noticed the almost imperceptible gesture and half smiled. He'd come a long, long way in the past fifteen years. Not only was San Francisco patrolman Adam Lassiter, badge number 801, now *Captain* Lassiter, he was also the head of the much-publicized California task force on organized crime.

He'd changed, she suspected, remembering the no-nonsense, often brutally blunt young policeman she'd met so many years ago. His ability to slip into a public persona of masculine authority actually appeared to be automatic. Without knowing exactly why, Kara was a bit saddened by the idea that he had changed so drastically.

"Hello," he called up to her, dropping his luggage with obvious relief onto the sparkling coral sand. "I'm looking for Colin Tiernan's cottage."

Of course he was. Remembering Colin's promise that he was sending her something special for yesterday's birthday, Kara vowed to give him a piece of her mind at the very first opportunity. As much as she dearly loved her older brother, Kara wished that he would abandon his campaign to marry her off.

Her calm voice betrayed none of her inner annoyance. "You've found it."

"Thank God. I was beginning to feel like Robinson Crusoe."

"It's one of the most deserted stretches of beach on Kauai," Kara acknowledged. "That's why Colin picked it. He values his privacy." She didn't add that the beach's remoteness had held the same appeal for her.

"I know about his penchant for being off the beaten track," Adam said with a smile. "His house in Big Sur is even more remote than this place. You practically need a mountain goat to climb up that road of his. . . . I'm forgetting my manners," he said suddenly. "I'm Adam Lassiter."

"Introductions aren't really necessary, Adam. Despite the fact that you've taken to dressing like an undertaker, I still recognize you."

He shaded his eyes with his hand as he looked up at her. There was something naggingly familiar about her. They'd met before, he determined, but as busy as his life had admittedly been, especially the past few months, Adam couldn't imagine how he had managed to forget this woman.

His studied gaze took in her slender face, her dark gray eyes, the cloud of fiery hair drifting over her shoulders. It was the hair that rang a bell. He forced his mind to concentrate, to remember.

Eventually, with effort, a vision appeared through the mist of Adam's memory. A hazy picture of a thirteen-year-old girl who'd surprised her older brother with a visit that long-ago Christmas: a young girl who had been less than pleased to discover that she would be sharing that brother with an outspoken rookie cop named Adam Lassiter.

The friendship between the fledgling novelist and the equally unseasoned patrolman, only six weeks out of the police academy, had begun purely by chance. Colin had been researching his first novel, and since his protagonist was to be a San Francisco patrolman, he had arranged to spend his nights riding along with one of San Francisco's finest.

After a week of boring, routine calls, the two young men had found themselves involved in a hair-raising adventure. The high-speed chase of an armed robbery suspect up and down the famed hills of San Francisco, which made every police movie they had ever seen pale by comparison, had ended abruptly at a warehouse on the Embarcadero, where the suspect took an elderly night watchman hostage. The standoff had gone on for hours before Adam was able to convince his superiors that he had learned his way around every inch of this particular warehouse while working on the loading dock to put himself through San Francisco University.

As the dawn broke on the horizon, Adam had crept stealthily through the shadows, managing both to free the watchman and apprehend the perpetrator, but not before receiving a twenty-two slug in the shoulder. The following week he'd been rewarded with a departmental commendation, Colin had enough material for ten books, and the kid sister had returned to Hawaii in a teenage huff.

No, Adam thought with a fleeting sense of awe. It couldn't be her.

"Kara?" he asked hesitatingly, still unable to accept this vision of femininity as Colin's skinny, redheaded, smart-mouthed kid sister.

"Got it on the first try. Congratulations. I was wondering if you'd make the connection."

"How could I forget you?" he hedged, not wanting to admit that he hadn't recognized her at first glance. That admission would lead to the less than complimentary implication that Kara Tiernan had changed dramatically over the past fifteen years.

"How indeed," she said with a silvery laugh that Adam suspected was directed at herself. "Especially after I succeeded in ruining your holidays."

"You weren't that bad. Besides, it was only natural that you'd resent Colin spending so much time with a stranger after you'd come all the way to California to be with him."

"Pooh," Kara protested with a wave of her hand, "you don't have to be so chivalrous, Adam. I was a brat."

With the 20/20 vision of hindsight, Kara had long ago realized that Colin's friend had done everything humanly possible to welcome her to San Francisco. He'd offered to take her to the zoo on his day off, but she had professed an allergy to wild animals. Chinatown was also out, Kara had insisted, firmly expressing a complete lack of interest in a part of the city she was secretly dying to see. Fisherman's Wharf? The smell of cooking crabs made her nauseated.

"I'm surprised you didn't toss me off the Golden Gate bridge," Kara admitted. A smile played at the corners of her full lips.

Adam suddenly recalled Kara's crashing the intimate little New Year's Eve party he and Colin had planned with two winsome and oh, so very willing Air France flight attendants.

"I thought about it a time or two."

Adam was stunned when he heard the admission escape his lips. He was usually a great deal more circumspect, weighing his words carefully when he represented the San Francisco Police Department, as well as the task force, to the press. More than one newsman had suggested that discretion flowed in Adam Lassiter's veins, right along with his blood. Adam himself knew differently, having spent years learning to censor his speech. Cops with runaway mouths never made captain. And they damned well didn't get the national exposure the task force had earned him.

To Adam's vast relief, Kara took no offense at his words. Instead, her laughter bubbled up like crystal water from a mountain stream. "What a relief to know that the outspoken Adam Lassiter I remember so well is lurking somewhere inside that funeral suit. I was afraid rubbing elbows with all those politicians might have ruined you."

"I haven't changed that much," he insisted, knowing it to be a lie. Sometimes lately he had found himself wondering if the kid who had crawled through those dark and threatening shadows in that warehouse so many years ago even existed any longer. "I'm still just a cop."

"You're a police captain," Kara argued. "And a very high-profile one, at that. I read all about your task force in *Time*. They also said that you're thinking about running for governor." There was an obvious question in her tone.

Adam's answer was short, succinct. "*Time*'s wrong." His blue eyes narrowed. "You know, you sound exactly like your brother; Colin doesn't much care for politicians, either."

"Family tradition," she murmured. Kara's expression immediately sobered as she gave him a long, thoughtful look. "But Colin would probably continue to like you even if you were running for office," she mused aloud. "There's only one man my brother would invite to stay at his house."

"Two."

"Two?"

The smile widened, dazzling in its wattage. Oh, yes, Kara decided, if he ever did run for office, this man would have one terrific future ahead of him. How many women would vote for Adam Lassiter solely on the strength of that smile and those gorgeous eyes?

"You're forgetting Captain Black."

Despite her irritation with his unexpected arrival, Kara chalked up a point for the man on a mental scoreboard. Colin had written her about his resident ghost, supposedly a sea captain whose ship had gone down on the rocks off the rugged California coast, making Kara wonder if Colin was simply getting too involved in his work. Fifteen years of writing occult novels could probably do that to you, she imagined.

She looked down at the man standing below her, trying to ignore the fact that his hair, in the bright sunshine, looked like spun gold.

"You sound as if you actually believe in ghosts." That was a surprise; she would have guessed Adam Lassiter to be too pragmatic an individual to dabble in fantasy.

"I didn't, but listening to Colin go on and on about the guy tends to make anyone a believer."

His mind returned to Colin Tiernan's effusive description of the island. One thing he obviously hadn't embellished was the beauty of at least one of its women. Kara's face had the kind of bone structure that made him wish his camera wasn't packed away in his luggage. He was going to photograph her, Adam decided, with the breeze ruffling her coppery hair, and the setting sun at her back. He squinted slightly as he imagined the scene, restraining the urge to frame it with his hands.

Her words broke into his consciousness, disturbing what had been evolving into a provocatively sensual mental image.

"Colin's got quite a talent for making even the most skeptical person believe in the supernatural," Kara agreed. "After he sent me the advance copy of *Nighthawk*, I locked my doors every night for a month."

He frowned at that. "You don't any longer?"

"This isn't San Francisco, Adam," Kara replied quietly. "We're not accustomed to much crime here in Kauai."

"True, but . . ." His voice trailed off, and he gave her another one of those brilliant, two-hundred-watt smiles. "You'll have to forgive me; every so often the cop in me comes to the surface."

"I suppose you would get a jaded view of the world after a while."

"It's not that bad; there are some advantages to working in a business where the customer is always wrong."

"If you say so," Kara murmured doubtfully. She picked up her hammer and slid it into a loop on the tool belt she wore low on her hips. "Why don't I come down so we can continue this conversation without your getting a crick in your neck?"

He moved to the side of the house in order to steady the ladder. Adam decided that the view, as Kara deftly backed down the aluminum steps, was as lovely as anything Colin could have promised. When she reached the ground, she turned, her hands splayed on her hips as she looked up at him.

The soft sea breeze ruffled her hair, giving him an indication of what she might look like immediately after making love. Adam was momentarily distracted by a strange urge to reach out and wrap a long titian curl around his hand. As they searched his, her smoky gray eyes turned suddenly skeptical.

"You're not in the market for a wife by any chance, are you?"

"Good Lord, no," Adam returned instantly.

Realizing how ungallant his swift rejection might have sounded, he sought to soften the denial. "You see, it's just that my life is quite complicated right now, and I don't believe I could give a relationship the time and energy . . ." His voice drifted off as Kara dissolved into gales of breathless laughter.

"Don't panic." Her merry grin moved to her eyes, lightening them to a gleaming pewter. "I was simply making certain that you weren't in on Colin's devious little plot."

"Plot?" A puzzled line appeared between his brows.

"My brother has been threatening to marry me off for the longest time," she said conversationally. As she bent to pick up his worn leather attaché case from the sand, the jeans rode up enticingly, momentarily capturing his attention.

"It's obvious that he sent you down here as bait." Kara picked up the smaller of the two pieces of luggage and a leather carryon bag and headed toward the front porch of the cottage.

"I don't think he'd do that," Adam objected. "Here, let me take those."

"Don't be silly. I'm far stronger than I look. You bring the large bag and that other case. What is it—a computer?"

"A lap-top portable," he acknowledged. "I thought that if this place was as peaceful as Colin promised, I might get some work done."

"You came here to work?" Kara's expression was incredulous.

"Something wrong with that?"

"Everyone's entitled to his own idiosyncrasies, I suppose."

Kara stopped and glanced back over her shoulder to give him a slow, appraising look. "Colin's told me all about you, Adam."

"No wonder my ears were burning; Colin is the only man on earth who knows all my peccadillos. If the press ever slips truth serum into those vats of coffee your brother consumes night and day, I'll be a goner."

"Oh, don't worry, my brother considers you to be intelligent, honest and a terrific judge of literature." Once again she flashed him that quick, bold grin. "That last is because you read all his books, of course."

"Of course," Adam murmured, still entranced by the power of Kara's sunshine smile. "So what other deep, dark secrets about my personal life has your brother let out of the bag?"

"He said you needed to relearn how to relax, which is probably the first thing my know-it-all brother and I have ever agreed about.... Watch that third step," she warned as she continued toward the front door. "It's loose. I was going to nail it down after I put in the skylight."

"Skylight?"

"Colin asked me to put one in for him; he also asked me to fix the place up." She entered the house, headed for what Adam assumed to be the bedroom. He had no choice but to follow.

"Of course," she continued blithely, "he didn't tell me that I was doing the remodeling for you, but as soon as I saw you struggling up the beach, I knew what my sneaky brother had in mind. He's obviously selected you as the likely candidate to save me from a lifetime of lonely, celibate spinsterhood."

Adam wondered if she was merely eccentric or charmingly mad. Whatever, he was intrigued. He also wondered exactly how celibate an existence the lovely Kara Tiernan actually led. Was there a man in her life, he wondered.

"Colin only offered me his house out of friendship. Not that you haven't grown into a remarkably attractive woman, Kara," he said sincerely, "but I'm not at all interested in marriage right now."

"That makes two of us," she said cheerfully. "Although I think we're in the minority these days, Adam. Even my best friend has fallen victim to the matrimonial bug; I'm going to be maid of honor at her wedding at the Fern Grotto next month and believe me, when she throws that bridal bouquet, I'm definitely going to duck.

"Not that I actually believe in that old wives' tale, of course, but there's no point in taking any unnecessary chances, is there? Well, welcome to Shangri-La."

Adam, following her, came to an abrupt halt in the doorway of the bedroom, his eyes widening as he took in the unexpected scene. Greenery filled the room—rubber trees, broad-leafed plants, vines—the number and variety too numerous to catalog. A king-size bed, draped in a bold, masculine fake-leopard-skin fur dominated the room. A broad beam of buttery sunshine from the overhead skylight cast a soft sheen on the fur and bathed the wide bed in a warm, inviting glow. The silvery sound of the water, tumbling over the lava stones, drew his attention to a fountain in a far corner of the vast room.

"It's certainly... inviting," he said, staring at the sybaritic scene.

"That's exactly what Colin had in mind," Kara said dryly. "Watch this."

She crossed the room, pulling the cord on the bamboo shades, to reveal a wall of glass. Outside, the soft sigh of the turquoise water, as it kissed the coral sand, enhanced the unabashed sensuality of the room's decor.

His imagination stimulated by the erotic atmosphere, Adam found the sight of Kara's firm, high breasts, barely concealed by her flowered bikini top, to be extremely, uncomfortably appealing. He dragged his gaze away and looked out the window.

"Your brother certainly thought of everything."

"He certainly did," Kara agreed. "Would you like to know when he requested this little rush remodeling job?" She answered her own question. "Last week. I've been working like a demon in order to get everything done on time."

Kara's words drew his eyes back to her, although this time Adam kept them steadfastly directed at her face, which didn't help his concentration any as he drank in the sight of her soft, smoky eyes, the thick lashes, and her full, lushly inviting lips. Surrounded by that thick mane of fiery hair, Kara Tiernan's face was that of a Homeric sea goddess. Adam was entranced. Reluctantly he forced his mind back to their conversation.

"You did all this?"

"I'm something of a local handyman," she said offhandedly. "By the way, the fur is definitely fake. I put my foot down at killing animals just so my dear brother could create a tropical version of the *Playboy* mansion."

She stuck her hands in her back pockets as she looked around the room. "Yes, I did all this with my own two hands at Colin's request, never realizing that I was setting the scene for my own seduction."

Adam Lassiter, to his knowledge, had never, in his thirty-six years, blushed, but as he felt the heat rising from the back of his collar, he realized that there was always a first time for everything.

"I think you're confused about my purpose in being here."

She eyed him consideringly. "Oh, I believe you when you say you're here in order to get some work done. But believe me, Colin has entirely different plans for us."

He shook his head. "Do all the Tiernans have such vivid imaginations?"

She waved away his protest. "I'll explain later. Right now, I need a shower and you need to get out of those city clothes. I'll meet you in thirty minutes over at my place."

"Your place?"

"Right around the bend." Kara pointed out the window to the curving white beach. "Handy, isn't it?" she said dryly. She paused on her way to the bedroom door and placed her hand on Adam's sleeve.

"Don't worry about it." She soothed him with a friendly smile that was obviously meant to reassure. "I have no intention of setting any feminine traps for you, Adam Lassiter. You're perfectly safe with me."

With that, she was gone, leaving Adam to stare out the expanse of glass, admiring the way her hips moved in those faded cutoff jeans. The tall, willowy redhead moved with the feral grace of a panther. Glancing down at the spot where her fingers had rested briefly on his arm, Adam imagined he could still feel the heat.

"I wonder," he murmured thoughtfully to himself.

He had a vague, uneasy feeling that he knew exactly how that other Adam must have felt when Eve suddenly showed up in Paradise.

2

"DON'T YOU OWN anything casual?"

Adam raised an argumentative brow. "What's wrong with this?"

Kara took a sip of iced pineapple juice as she slowly, judiciously studied the man sitting across from her. He had changed out of the charcoal gray business suit, but the bark-brown slacks, cream-colored silk shirt and subtly striped tie were still a far cry from appropriate beach attire. As her eyes moved to his feet, she supposed the supple Italian loafers were Adam Lassiter's attempt at informality and wondered what had happened to those raggedy old Nikes he had practically lived in while off duty.

"In the first place, that tie has to go. No one, I repeat, no one, wears a tie on Kauai."

He narrowed his eyes. "I'm not accustomed to running with the pack."

Kara had to give him credit for the way he stated that simple, obvious fact. He had avoided sounding unbearably egocentric, the way most men of his vast accomplishments invariably did.

"That's undoubtedly true," she agreed. "However, when in Rome . . ." She reached over, her fingers extricating him from the narrow strip of silk. "That's better, but you still need more work," she murmured as she unfastened the top two buttons of his shirt.

The same heat Adam had felt earlier on his arm moved to his throat as Kara fiddled with his collar, exposing his skin to the tropical sun.

"You know, I could learn to enjoy this," he said. "When do we get to the part where I undress you?"

His deep, seductive tone made Kara's fingers freeze on the creamy silk. For a brief moment, she felt herself drowning in the deep blue pools of Adam's eyes. Instinct warned her to keep things light. She smiled, with a slow, tantalizing curve of her lips that Adam found vastly fascinating.

"Aren't you rushing things a bit, Mr. Lassiter?" she asked smoothly.

A random breeze feathered her hair across her cheek. Adam pushed it aside in a casual gesture that didn't fool either one of them. "Am I?" he asked, his gaze fixed on her face.

Even in the unforgiving light of the bright Hawaiian sun, her skin was flawless, her eyes the color of wood smoke in autumn. When those dark eyes widened in response to his finger trailing down her jaw, Adam could feel the heat rise.

As he leaned toward her, Adam was all male energy, barely restrained. Kara wondered if he were even capable of relaxing. So far, the man hadn't even loosened up enough to slouch.

"We tend to take things a little more slowly down here than you're used to in the big city."

Adam had learned early in his career the advantage of maintaining eye contact during the most casual-seeming of conversations. The technique had invariably worked, giving him an unprecedented confession record.

"Believe me, Kara," he murmured, "even in the city, there are certain things I prefer to do very, very slowly."

Even as Kara found herself being seduced against her will by his resonant velvety voice and lustrous blue eyes, she was pleased to discover him to be a man of contradictions. Who could have suspected that anyone who insisted on wearing a tie in the islands could be so marvelously, enticingly sexy?

Kara had always enjoyed surprises; she had always found pleasure in the unexpected. And Adam Lassiter definitely filled the bill. The trick, she reminded herself firmly, was in knowing how to handle him. Kara Tiernan had not reached the ripe old age of twenty-eight without having had plenty of practice in the care and handling of the opposite sex.

"You've no idea how glad I am to hear that, Adam," she said brightly. "Then you'll undoubtedly understand when I take tomorrow off in order to run a few personal errands instead of fixing your roof as I had originally planned."

Instead of being annoyed by the way she had so deftly slipped the net of desire that had suddenly surrounded them, Adam threw back his head and laughed. Kara decided she liked the sound—liked it a lot.

"What if it rains?" he countered, once he'd stopped laughing.

"It probably will," she assured him airily. "This place isn't called the Garden Island for nothing. It takes a lot of moisture to grow all these gorgeous flowers."

"And if my roof leaks?"

Kara sighed exaggeratedly as she placed her glass on the bamboo table beside her. She left the porch for a moment, returning with a steel bucket emblazoned with red and yellow hand-painted flowers.

"Here you go," she said, holding it out to him as she sat down. "Now you're well covered. If you get more leaks, Colin undoubtedly has plenty of pots and pans that'll do in a pinch."

Adam knew without asking that Kara was responsible for the artwork on the bucket. "You seem to have everything covered."

"Not quite everything," she murmured.

She frowned as she leaned back in the wicker chair and propped her feet on the porch railing. Adam noticed that her slender legs, clad in a pair of brief white shorts, seemed to go on forever.

Kara's own slow, judicious gaze went from the top of Adam's blond head down to his loafer-clad feet. "What time do you want to go shopping?"

He arched a golden brow. "Shopping?"

"For clothes. Honestly, Adam, you can't possibly hope to enjoy yourself dressed like an escapee from Wall Street."

A scarlet bougainvillea blossom floated down from a brilliant branch overhead, landing on Kara's thigh to contrast vividly with her golden skin. As she absently flicked the flower away, Adam's attention was drawn once again to that smooth expanse of skin. It took an effort, but he managed to keep the sound of desire from his smooth tone.

"I've been assured that the proper choice in clothing encourages respect."

Kara observed him unblinkingly over the rim of her glass as she took a sip of her juice. "If you need a dark suit in order to earn respect, you're probably in trouble," she said. "Why don't you just admit it, Adam? The suit looks a lot better on television than the T-shirt and faded jeans I remember you wearing."

His smile didn't dim in wattage, but his eyes became shuttered with a skill Kara couldn't help but admire. She had never been able to develop that particular talent.

"I didn't realize you'd been paying so much attention to my attire. In fact, I got the impression that you couldn't stand to be in the same room with me," he said quietly.

Kara shrugged. "I didn't like you," she admitted. "I never said that you weren't good-looking."

Adam was surprised by the pleasure her soft admission brought him. "But not anymore?" he prompted.

Her gray eyes examined him in a way that was not at all encouraging. "You're still a very attractive man, Adam," she said slowly.

"But?"

She shook her head. "You're slicker than you used to be. It's as if after hanging around all those politicians, you've picked up some of their veneer."

"Meaning I've turned into a phony?"

Kara had the good grace to blush. Why on earth did she keep insulting the man? After all, he was Colin's best friend. The least she could do is show a little aloha spirit.

"I seem to be doing it again, don't I?" When his raised eyebrow invited elaboration, Kara continued. "Behaving like a spoiled, sharp-tongued brat. Really, Adam, I apologize. I don't know what got into me."

"You've probably had a long day," he suggested helpfully.

"That's probably it," Kara mumbled, not wanting to contradict him, for that would entail admitting that something about Adam Lassiter put her nerves uncharacteristically on edge. She fell silent as they both stared out over the turquoise water.

"Colin assured me that this was the ideal place to unwind," Adam said at length.

"And you need to unwind." It was not a question.

Adam attempted a smile that turned into a grimace instead. "Is it that obvious? You needn't bother to answer," he said swiftly, holding up a hand. "I don't know if my ego could take any more battering right now."

Kara thought about that for a moment, wondering if he was serious about her ability to hurt him. Surely he was exaggerating. Wasn't he?

"Well, you certainly can't relax in a suit and tie," she pointed out finally. She ran her hand through her wild mass of reddish gold hair and narrowed her eyes as she studied him thoughtfully. "Blue, I think," she mused aloud.

Kara nodded, satisfied. "Yes, blue will do very nicely. A deep sapphire shade to match your eyes. Of course you know that they're quite remarkable."

Adam was used to playing games with women; he was adept at saying the right things at the right time. But never had he met anyone quite like Kara. Her candor was as refreshing as it was unnerving.

"Are they?"

"Of course they are," she said, tossing her head. "For heaven's sake, Adam, an intelligent man, especially one who's beginning to receive national attention, has certainly taken time to enumerate his strengths and weaknesses. And your eyes are definitely one of the nicest things about you."

She leaned forward to study them more closely, her own eyes narrowed thoughtfully. "They're actually a great deal like Colin's, but of course his are lighter, more like blue ice. Yours remind me of the sea at midnight, under a full moon."

She gave him another of those slow smiles that caused an odd tingling at the base of his spine. "It's too bad you're not going to run for governor; you'd probably get the women's vote solely on the strength of those gorgeous blue eyes."

At any other time he would have hurriedly assured Kara that were he running for office, which he most definitely wasn't, he would want to win on the issues, not on the color of his eyes. But all Adam could think of at that moment was that her smiling lips were only a whisper away. He could feel her breath, like a soft summer breeze against his mouth. All he'd have to do would be to lean forward, the slightest bit, and . . .

"Oh, no!" Kara jumped to her feet, frantically looking down at the wide diver's watch strapped to her wrist. "I completely lost track of the time. He's going to be absolutely livid! Damn. I hate having to listen to a lecture on punctuality."

Leaving Adam to stare after her, she dashed into the weathered clapboard house, and seconds later came out with a small brown bag clutched in her hand.

"Dinner's at eight," she called back as she jogged backward down the beach. "Since you don't know the way, I'll pick you up."

Before Adam could ask what had just happened, Kara had turned the corner and disappeared from view. Only the lingering, evocative scent of frangipani proved that the blithe spirit with the smoky eyes and fiery hair had been anything more than a particularly enticing figment of his imagination.

THAT EVENING Adam sat on the lanai of the cottage, watching as the setting sun turned the sky to apricot, the sea to beaten gold in a moment of timeless beauty. Colin had been right about the tranquillity, he mused, gazing out at the pristine beach colored by a mist-softened sunset. Almost in spite of himself, he had begun to relax. It felt good, he admitted almost reluctantly. When was the last time he had taken a vacation? He could barely remember.

His pleasant state of lassitude halted abruptly as Kara came around the cove, appearing like something from a fairy tale. Or a midnight fantasy. Her hair, gilded by the last rays of the sun and fanned by the soft trade winds, was adorned with a bright yellow blossom. A dress with spaghetti straps and covered with bright tropical flowers bared her sun-kissed shoulders and skimmed her body enticingly, the full skirt blowing around her legs as she walked.

In her hand she carried a pair of sandals. When she reached the bottom of the steps, she stopped and smiled. Desire slammed into him.

Kara's smile altered subtly as she found herself responding to the sudden heat of Adam's dark blue eyes. "I hope you're hungry."

Not one to hammer home a point, Adam didn't pick up on the obvious. "Starved," he admitted, willing to allow the sensual moment to fade. For the moment. "Where are we going?"

Timing. The man definitely had it. Kara chalked up yet another point in his favor on her mental scoreboard as she pushed her windblown hair out of her eyes. "Didn't I tell you?"

"You were in a bit of a hurry," Adam pointed out. "Did you get your lecture?"

"Lecture?" She blew her bangs from her eyes. "Oh, that. Yes, I had to listen for an interminably long time to how I must pay more attention to detail. Actually it was rather annoying, being treated like a child. Especially by a fish."

Adam lifted a questioning brow. "A fish?"

"Moby Dick," she murmured, brushing a few strands of flyaway hair out of her eyes. "And a foul-tempered old thing he is, too. I believe I'm just going to stop visiting him if he can't treat me with more respect...."

"I'm going to do it," she vowed suddenly. "First thing tomorrow. No more vacillating. I'm simply going to do it."

Adam struggled to keep up with the sudden conversational detour. "Do what?"

"Cut my hair, of course," she said. She nodded emphatically. "In fact, I believe I'll do it now. No sense putting off until tomorrow something you can do tonight, as some sickeningly efficient person once said."

She started up the steps. "Do you happen to have a pair of scissors in the house? Surely you do; Colin is always clipping his reviews. Not that he ever reads them. My brother doesn't approve of book reviewers, but he does enjoy seeing his name in print. He and I are different in that way, of course—not that anyone would ever want to write anything about me."

Adam caught her arm as she passed him. Her smooth, tanned skin was as soft as he had thought it would be. A sultry, tropical fragrance teased his nose.

"I can't let you do this, Kara."

She looked up at him, clearly surprised. "For heaven's sake, Adam Lassiter, what on earth do you have to say about the way I wear my hair?" She grabbed a handful of the thick reddish curls and held it up in front of his face.

"Do you have any idea how much trouble this stuff is? I have to wash it twice a day when I go snorkeling, it's hot, heavy, it's forever blowing in my eyes, and when I do try to tie it out of the way, it'll never stay where I want it to, and—"

"I like it just the way it is." He reached out, running the silky strands through his fingers as if he were sifting sand.

Kara fell silent, her eyes locked with his. The man was remarkable: he hadn't even raised his voice, yet the command was unmistakable. Despite her irritation that he would presume to make such a demand, Kara found herself admiring his silent power of intimidation. She was beginning to understand what Colin had in common with Adam Lassiter. Both men were obviously used to getting their own way.

"What you like," she said smoothly, "doesn't really have any bearing on this case, Captain. However, since I've already had to listen to one annoying lecture on my lack of punctuality today, I'm not going to waste time cutting my hair right now. It would only make us late to dinner. I'll simply save it for tomorrow morning."

"That's better."

He released her hair, rubbing his hands together as if he had never expected any other outcome. They had gone a little way down the beach when his next words brought her to an abrupt stop.

"Of course, now I'll have to think of ways to keep you occupied until you get that ridiculous notion out of your head."

"It's not a ridiculous notion. Oh, it's all right for you to say," she snapped, her flashing eyes moving to his short blond hair. "A quick dip under the shower, two swipes with a comb, and you're presentable. Well, let me tell you, Adam Lassiter, it's not that easy."

"Indulge me," he said, putting his hand on her back as they started walking again. "All afternoon I've entertained a fantasy of running my fingers through those lush, thick curls while we're making love."

Kara had not been unaware of the attraction; it was, after all, mutual. Something about him had affected her from that very first moment, and as a creature of impulse, Kara was accustomed to following her instincts. Still, the casual, offhand way Adam stated his thoughts caught her off guard. She would have expected him to be more cautious, more circumspect.

She gave him a long, considering look. "Pretty sure of yourself, aren't you, Captain Lassiter?"

Adam's gaze lowered to her lips, then returned to her dusky eyes. "Would you rather play games?" His look was surprisingly reasonable, considering the suddenly provocative topic of conversation.

In spite of the excitement rippling through her, or perhaps because of it, Kara kept her tone even. "I've always enjoyed games."

"As long as they're played by your rules," he guessed.

She gave him a flash of a smile. "Of course."

If there was one thing Adam had never been able to ignore, it was a challenge. His hands cupped her shoulders, creating a surging heat as they slid slowly down her arms. When he had linked their fingers together, he lifted her right hand to his lips.

"I think," he said softly, brushing her skin with a feathery kiss that made her pulse leap in response, "that this could be a very interesting vacation."

A hint of amusement showed in her mouth. *Oh, Colin,* Kara thought, *you do know how to tempt a person.* It was an intriguing feeling, this unexpected attraction. The fact that it had been so instantaneous, for a man with whom she could never, under any circumstances, become emotionally involved, made it even more surprising.

"Or a long one, at any rate," she countered dryly.

He laughed at that, suddenly finding pleasure in everything. In the balmy trade winds, the tranquil picture-postcard setting, and most of all, the company.

"Where are we going?" he asked once again, after they'd continued their slow walk up the beach in silence. She had offered no objection to his continuing to hold her hand, which was fine with him, since Adam was in no hurry to relinquish possession.

"My parents' house. Tonight is something of a command performance for me, and since I didn't think Colin would approve of my leaving you to spend your first night on the island alone, I figured the best thing to do would be to take you along."

"Are you sure they won't mind?"

She looked at him curiously. "Why on earth would they mind?"

He shrugged. "Well, if it's a special occasion—"

"Don't be silly," she broke in with a rippling laugh that again reminded him of a crystal mountain stream. "It's only another one of Daddy's unveiling ceremonies." In the soft light her eyes gleamed with amusement. "He assures me that he's created yet another masterpiece."

"I thought your father was a doctor."

"He is. One of those old-fashioned family practitioners. Oh, look!" she exclaimed suddenly, pointing up at the top of the jagged cliff rising inland, shrouded in silver mist and softened by the touch of a rainbow. "Make a wish."

"Why?"

Her look was one of sheer frustration. "Because of the rainbow, of course." She closed her eyes. "Hurry, before it disappears."

Feeling undeniably foolish, Adam found himself doing as he was bidden. But wishing that he was making love to Kara Tiernan was certainly no hardship.

"There," she said with satisfaction, opening her eyes again. "I feel lucky tonight. I hope you wished for something wonderful, Adam, because I just know it will come true."

"So do I," he agreed, vowing that whatever other decisions he reached about his life during the next few weeks, he was definitely going to have Kara. "I thought it was the first star people wished on."

"That only happens once a day," she explained blithely. "If you wish on rainbows, sometimes you get a chance for two or three wishes every day. The odds are much better."

Before he could respond to that, a huge beast the size of a small horse came bounding down the beach, a long pink tongue lolling from its mouth. A moment later, the beast, which turned out to be a boisterous Harlequin Great Dane, stood on his hind legs, his huge paws braced on Kara's bare shoulders as he joyfully licked her face.

"Meet Horatio," she said, appearing unperturbed as she brushed wet sand off the front of her dress. "Horatio, this is Mr. Lassiter. He's a very good friend of Colin's, so I want you to treat him like one of the family."

She bent and picked up a piece of driftwood, throwing it down the beach. Horatio took off after it, barking enthusiastically.

"He's spoiled rotten, of course," she said as they watched the dog splashing in the surf as he attempted to retrieve the stick. "So you'd best humor him. It's all Daddy's fault."

"He's your father's dog, then?"

"In a way. You see, Daddy always wanted four children—two sons and two daughters, but mother felt one of each should be enough for any family." She grinned. "Especially when the two children in question were so amazingly exemplary."

"They are definitely that," he agreed, returning her smile.

Kara's eyes danced merrily. "Thank you, Adam. That was precisely what you were supposed to say. Anyway," she said, picking up the threads of the story, "a few months ago, Daddy found Horatio at the animal shelter.

"He's adopted," she said under her breath as the huge black-and-white animal came bounding back, the stick between his wide jaws. "But no one has had the heart to tell him. He's really very sensitive."

"Are you telling me—"

She pressed her fingers against his lips. "Shh," she murmured hurriedly, "while I don't entirely agree with Daddy on the subject, I respect his right to keep the facts of Horatio's adoption from him. For the time being."

She reached down and patted the happily panting dog on the head. "After all, he is only a puppy. When he's older, he'll be able to understand much better."

Adam searched her face for a hint of humor and found none. He wondered why Colin had never told him that his sister was slightly off kilter. Then, thinking of Colin Tiernan, living in a haunted house with the ghost of a sea captain for a roommate while he wrote lurid tales about things that go bump in the night, Adam realized Colin had undoubtedly never noticed. Obviously the Tiernan family had a looser standard than the rest of the world when it came to describing normalcy.

"Whatever you do," she warned as they approached the sprawling, weathered house perched high atop the oceanside cliff, "don't tell Daddy I told you about Horatio. He's always been very protective of his children, and he probably wouldn't appreciate my telling family secrets."

"I promise not to breathe a word," Adam said solemnly.

Kara had known Adam had possibilities. She rewarded him with a broad smile. "You are a nice man, Adam Lassiter," she said. "I think I just may forgive my brother for sending you down here to seduce me, after all."

Standing on her toes, she brushed her lips against his. Adam felt a flash of heat and flame before she broke the all-too-brief contact.

His hands settled firmly on her slender hips, holding her when she would have moved away. "My turn," he said softly.

As his lips covered hers, Kara reminded herself that she had been prepared for this kiss. That in truth she had initiated it. But nothing could have prepared her for the whirlwind effect it had on her senses. His hand tangled in her hair, his long fingers pressing against the back of her head, as if forestalling her escape—not that she had the slightest intention of moving.

His mouth was not harsh, but neither was it gentle as he claimed hers as if it were his perfect right. The tip of his tongue traced her lips with a circle of lightning; she parted them with a soft sigh. When his teeth nibbled enticingly at her lower lip, Kara responded out of sheer pleasure, raising her arms to put them around his neck. At the feel of her slender curves against his body, Adam groaned, deepening the kiss, taking her on a roller-coaster ride of emotions.

Kara clung to him, her own avid lips now moving under his, tasting, teasing, delighting in the thrilling ascent as he took her higher and higher with only the expertise of his kiss. It was as if every nerve ending in her body was focused on her mouth, leaving Kara stunned by how exciting a mere kiss could be.

Adam had wanted women before, probably with the same intensity as he had been wanting Kara since he had first spotted her, seated like a scantily clad nymph atop his roof. Accustomed to achieving whatever he set out to do, he had known he was going to taste her before the evening was out. That had been a foregone conclusion long before she had shown up at his cottage looking and smelling as if she had just stepped out of the enchanted forest.

But he hadn't expected what should have been a standard, experimental kiss to have such a devastating effect on his senses. There was a roar inside his head like the crashing of surf, and his body was infused with a slow, deep ache. Although he was used to controlling every aspect of his life, Adam suddenly felt as if he were slowly, inexorably, sinking into quicksand.

3

"WELL, WELL," a feminine voice said with a low, deep chuckle, "I see you've brought along another art lover for the unveiling."

Kara tilted her head back, her eyes smiling into Adam's as she slowly, reluctantly broke the heated contact.

"Mother," she said, not taking her gaze from his, "meet Adam Lassiter. Adam, this is my mother."

Adam looked past Kara to a woman who, though taller than her daughter, had the same smoky, mischievous eyes. Unlike Kara's wild reddish mane, however, her jet black hair flowed down her back like a rippling waterfall, brightened here and there by brilliant streaks of silver.

Her flowing chiffon caftan was every bit as colorful as the tropically flowered dress worn by her daughter and her scent, if muskier, was enticing. Taking in the sight of mother and daughter, Adam felt as if he'd stumbled into a particularly delightful garden.

"It's a pleasure to meet you, Mrs. Tiernan," he said, struggling with an atypical embarrassment. How long had it been since he'd been caught making love to a woman by her parent? Years.

Althea Tiernan's brightly interested eyes moved from Adam to her daughter and back again. "The pleasure is ours, Adam," she said easily. "Colin has told us so much about you."

"Colin sent Adam down here to seduce me," Kara offered.

"Your brother has always been an enterprising man." Althea agreed easily. "In that respect he takes after your father."

Adam felt obliged to set the record straight. "Kara has things a little confused," he objected.

Althea smiled, the same slow, devastating smile that made her daughter so dangerous. "On the contrary, Adam," she corrected smoothly, "I'd say my daughter is quite perceptive." She glanced at Kara. "By the way, Liz called here looking for you; she sounded quite upset. I told her you'd call her back as soon as you arrived."

"Liz is my friend who's getting married," Kara explained to Adam. "She's been floating on clouds these past weeks; I wonder what could be wrong," she murmured, more to herself than to her mother or Adam.

"Perhaps she's called off the wedding," Althea suggested.

Kara shook her head decisively. "Not a chance. I've never seen a couple as wild about each other as Liz and Brett." She smiled up at her mother. "Except you and Daddy, of course."

Althea grinned at that. "What a nice thing to say," she enthused. "And so very true."

She moved aside, gesturing them into the house. The entry floor was covered in hemp-textured rugs, and track lighting along the ceiling illuminated the vivid paintings crowding the stark white walls. All were island scenes, the subjects varying from sun-dappled landscapes to formal portraits to colorful abstracts. The only thing the works of art had in common was that they were undeniably terrible. It was all Adam could do not to stop and stare.

"Did you warn Adam about the showing?" Althea asked Kara as they wound their way down the rambling hallway.

"I started to, but I got distracted by a rainbow."

"Oh, dear," Althea murmured regretfully, "I missed that one."

She looked up at Adam, whose attention had been momentarily captured by a portrait of a young native girl seated in the surf beside a wind-tossed palm. Had she stood up, Adam would have bet she'd have topped the tree by at least ten feet. He vaguely remembered seeing the portrait's twin in the airport terminal.

"I do hope you made a good wish, Adam," Althea said conversationally. "Evening rainbows are especially lucky, you know."

His eyes moved to Kara's. "I certainly hope so," he said huskily. The message that passed between them was unmistakable.

Althea nodded, satisfied. "Good. Now about Michael's painting," she said briskly. "It undoubtedly has not escaped your notice that my husband, while being both a delightful as well as intelligent man, possesses absolutely no talent whatsoever."

"His paintings are definitely unusual," Adam offered, not wanting to offend his hostess.

"Piffle," Kara declared. "My father and I just happen to be the only two individuals in this family who managed to be out to lunch when talent was being passed out. Unfortunately, while I accepted that fact long ago, Daddy continues to delude himself with the idea that he's another Gauguin."

"You're quite talented, Kara," Althea argued. "None of my friends' children have nearly as many college degrees as you've managed to obtain. And everyone loves what you've done to the house."

"Poor Mother." Kara grinned up at Adam. "She just can't accept the fact that she gave birth to a child with absolutely no artistic abilities."

Althea Tiernan's words reminded Adam of Colin's saying that Kara had stayed in school much longer than the average student, gathering degrees in history, comparative literature, philosophy and Russian studies. Colin had laughed at the time, remarking that his baby sister was probably the most overeducated unemployable person in the country.

"Don't be so hard on yourself, Kara," Adam advised lazily. "It's obvious to me that you're a woman of vast hidden talents."

His deep, sexy tone, when they had been speaking in such a casual manner, shook Kara to the core. *Oh, please,* she made a hasty, fervent wish, *don't let me fall in love. Not now. Not with this man.*

Seeing the distress on her daughter's face, Althea took pity on Kara and deftly returned the conversation to its original track. "My husband enjoys his little fantasy," she said with a graceful shrug, "so we all indulge him."

"'All' meaning the entire island," he guessed, thinking back on the painting in the airport.

"Of course," Kara broke in. "Daddy's treated everyone on Kauai at one time or another. Everybody adores him, so whenever he has a showing, people show up and buy out the gallery."

Adam tried to imagine such a communal act of subterfuge taking place in San Francisco and found it impossible. He felt as if his plane had somehow gone off course on the way down here and landed in Oz.

"Don't worry, Adam," Althea said with a deep, throaty laugh. She patted his cheek with fingertips that were roughened from years of sculpting stone and clay. "No one expects you to buy anything."

"Unless you want to," Kara hinted broadly. "Who knows, Adam, you might actually fall in love with Daddy's latest artistic effort and simply have to have it."

"It's Kara's turn to take a painting home," Althea explained.

"Well, I don't think it's fair," Kara grumbled. "Just because I live on the island, I have to hang the stuff on my walls. Colin stores his in the backs of his closets."

"You don't know that for a fact, Kara."

Kara looked knowingly at Adam. "You've visited Colin at home, haven't you?"

"Several times."

"So have you seen any Michael Tiernan paintings hanging around my brother's haunted house?"

"No," he admitted. "But I'm certain there's a good reason."

She folded her arms. "Name one."

"Perhaps Morgan Black took them."

At the mention of her son's uninvited houseguest, Althea looked interested. "Oh, have you met Colin's ghost friend, Adam?"

Adam was not nearly as surprised by the question as he might have been a few hours earlier. After hearing the story of Horatio, he had made the decision to simply go with the flow and not attempt to analyze anything having to do with the Tiernan family.

"Not yet. He seems to be rather reclusive."

"I suppose I can understand that," Althea mused. "However, it's not exactly the behavior you'd expect from a sea captain, now, is it? One would expect such a man to be far more gregarious."

She shook her head resignedly. "Oh, well, I'm certain that once he gets used to Colin's company, he'll open up."

They had reached a set of sliding doors that led to a flower-filled courtyard. At their arrival, an enormous orange cat sleeping on a bamboo throne chair lifted her head. Obviously deciding they weren't worth the effort it would take to wake up, she closed her amber eyes, dismissing them by flicking her striped tail over her nose.

"Kara!" A tall, silver-haired man rose from a wicker chair and came toward them, his tanned face wreathed in a welcoming smile. "You're a vision of loveliness tonight," he said, giving her a heartfelt embrace.

After he'd released his daughter, Michael Tiernan's bright blue eyes narrowed thoughtfully. "I do believe I'll paint you, my dear, wearing that very dress." He rubbed his chin. "We'll want the correct light, of course. Sunrise, I should think."

He nodded with satisfaction. "Definitely sunrise. It will bring out the fire in your hair."

"You know how much I adore you, Papa," Kara said firmly, "but if you expect me to pose for you before noon, you're crazy."

"Humph." He turned his attention to Adam. "What do you think?" he demanded. "Aren't I right? She should be painted with the first fingers of dawn rising over her shoulder."

"And her titian hair blowing free in the wind, like a wayward sea sprite," Adam agreed.

Michael clapped. "Exactly." He leaned forward, lifting her hair in soft clouds that drifted over her bare shoulders.

"Father," she said sternly, backing away, "that's enough for now."

For some strange reason she suddenly felt uncomfortable, submitting to Adam's unwavering gaze as her father discussed her as if she were nothing more than some inanimate object he intended to paint. She'd seen him look that same way at a pear. Or a tree. Or a fish, during his Hawaiian marine life stage.

He waved away her protest with a flick of his hand. "Don't disturb me when my muse is visiting, daughter." He fluffed her hair artistically, then turned to Adam. "Something's missing," he complained.

Adam considered his action for only a moment. Deciding he had nothing to lose, he said, "Let me try."

Before Kara could perceive his intent, he'd gathered her into his arms, kissing her heatedly until her head whirled. She was still dizzy when he released her.

"How's that?"

Michael clapped him on the shoulder. "My boy, you're an absolute genius. You must be a fellow painter."

"The only painting I've ever done is my apartment walls, and even that turned out rather badly. But I enjoy photography. In fact, I'd been planning much the same pose for Kara."

That was certainly news to her.

Kara's father nodded sagely. "Photography's much the same as painting, just a different medium. I can always recognize another kindred spirit. I'm Michael Tiernan."

"Adam Lassiter," Adam introduced himself. "Are you the same Michael Tiernan who painted the woman in the airport?"

"Saw it, did you?" Michael said with obvious pride. "What did you think?"

"I can honestly say I've never seen anything like it."

Kara hadn't realized she had been holding her breath until she exhaled a sigh of relief. Despite her irritation at the way he'd just manipulated her feelings for his own amusement, she gave Adam a faintly appreciative smile.

"I like this one," Michael announced. "Where have you been hiding him, Kara?"

"San Francisco," she answered absently, her eyes moving toward the draped easel in the corner. It was so big. Why couldn't her father take up painting miniatures? "Colin sent him to me for my birthday."

Michael nodded in much the same manner his wife had, on hearing the news. "Colin always did have exquisite taste in gifts. What will you have to drink, Adam, my boy?"

"Scotch, straight up, if you have it," Adam answered, tired of trying to explain his relationship with Kara. Besides, his steadfast denial had begun to ring false, even to his own ears.

"One Scotch, coming right up. No peeking!" Michael's deep voice boomed suddenly, causing Kara to jerk her fingers away from the edge of the white sheet. "We'll have the unveiling in due course. After dinner. A little suspense will heighten the appreciation."

He put his arm around Adam's shoulder. "In the meantime, why don't you help your mother in the kitchen, my dear, while your young man and I discuss the merits of early morning light."

He led Adam over to the pair of chairs. "Tallulah, it's time for you to join the ladies in the kitchen." he instructed firmly.

The orange tabby opened one yellow eye and looked up at him, apparently unmoved by his request.

"Come along, Tallulah dear," Althea coaxed, "we're having salmon tonight, and I believe I have an extra steak just for you."

She had said the magic words. The cat stretched in a slow, fluid movement, then jumped lightly onto the floor and followed the two women out of the room.

"Tallulah's a good girl," Michael said, watching the cat leave. "But stubborn. When she digs her claws in, she can give Kara a run for her money, and Lord knows, that one has been known to try a man's patience from time to time."

Of that Adam had not a single doubt. "Tallulah's your daughter?" he asked politely, remembering what Kara had told him about Michael Tiernan's desire for two sons and two daughters. If the man was off center enough to consider Horatio the second son he'd never had, it was only reasonable to assume that Kara's father thought of the huge orange cat as an equal member of the family.

Michael's face registered surprise as he handed Adam his drink. "Good God, man, what can you be thinking of? Any fool can see that's a cat."

THE NIGHT was gleaming silver and black velvet, as stars glistened in an ebony sky and indigo clouds scudded across the moon. The intoxicating scent of plumeria, oleander and sandalwood drifted on the warm Pacific breeze as the coral sand sparkled like diamonds underfoot.

"I like your family," Adam said as they returned down the beach after dinner.

"They like you, too."

"Even Horatio?"

The dog hadn't left Adam's side the entire time he was at the house. "Especially Horatio."

"You were pulling my leg with that bit about him being the other son your father never had, weren't you?" Adam asked casually.

Her eyes sparkled as brightly as the stars overhead as she looked up at him. "Guilty," she admitted, a runaway smile quirking the corners of her lips. "But I had you going for a moment, didn't I?"

"More than a moment. You should have seen your father's face when I asked him if Tallulah was his daughter."

Kara stared at him. A second later Adam decided that her breathless laughter was one of the most enticing things he'd ever heard.

"Oh, no," she gasped, pressing her fingers against her lips in an attempt to stop the out-of-control giggles, "you didn't."

"I certainly did," Adam said. "Your father looked at me as if I'd lost my mind."

"I told you not to mention it to him," Kara reminded Adam with a grin. "But you needn't worry; my father is a very tolerant man."

The warm water lapped against their legs as they waded in the foaming surf. She'd been secretly pleased when Adam had taken off his loafers to join her. Sometime during the day Kara had decided to make Adam Lassiter her new project. She would, she vowed, teach him to relax and learn to enjoy the simpler things in life.

"And of course my brother thinks you walk on water."

"The feeling's mutual." He felt the wet sand shift underfoot and tried to remember the last time he had done something as simple as walking along the beach. "I've been a fan of Colin's for a long time, ever since he rode around with me researching *The Haunting of Hannah Grimm*."

"My brother has a great many fans. He's choosier about his friends. He has to be."

Kara had not been away from California so long that she couldn't remember all those insincere people fawning over her brother. Movie studio executives, who saw a gold mine in his vastly popular occult novels. Starlets, would-be starlets and established stars, all wanting to be seen with the country's hottest novelist. Not to mention all those entrepreneurs wanting licensing rights for everything from the she-wolf vampire dolls to a Day-glo poster series depicting the savagely avenging spirits of a fictional California serial killer's victims.

Adam thought he detected a challenge in Kara's smooth tone. "I'm choosy about my friends, as well," he said easily. "I have to be."

With that point silently acknowledged, Kara decided to change the subject. "You don't have to keep the painting," she murmured. "That was a dirty trick."

He grinned at the memory. "Giving it to me as a welcome-to-Hawaii gift? I thought it was rather inspired."

She laughed softly. "It was the only thing I could think of. The minute I saw it, I knew I'd simply die if I had to hang it on my wall." She shook her head with good-natured regret. "I do wish my father would get over his Picasso period. At least in the old days his subjects bore some slight resemblance to reality."

"It is a little confusing," Adam agreed, thinking back on the brilliant orange-and-red abstract painting they had left at the Tiernans'. Michael had promised to have it delivered to Colin's cottage the following day.

"It's supposed to be the legend of Haena Beach."

"I'm still lost."

"It's one of the ancient legends this island thrives on," she explained. "One day, Pele, goddess of volcanoes, returned to Haena Beach when a great ceremony was in progress. As she watched the festivities, she was captivated by Lohiau, the handsome young chief in charge of the ceremony."

"Love at first sight," Adam murmured.

"Or at least lust at first sight," Kara agreed dryly. "Anyway, being a very passionate goddess, Pele decided that she had to have him, but there was only one slight problem."

The lazy breeze coming off the water fanned her hair, allowing him to breathe in the fragrant gardenia scent of her shampoo. Hit with a sudden jolt of desire, he slipped his free hand into his pocket to keep from touching her.

"A problem?" Adam wondered if she could hear in his voice the unsteadiness he was feeling.

Kara had. She stopped momentarily, looking up at him. In the silver moonlight her eyes shone like polished pewter. "Adam?"

He knew that if he responded to the soft invitation in her voice, he'd be a goner. Patience, he reminded himself. Control and patience. He'd built his life on those solid foundations and he wasn't about to allow this woman to undermine them in a single day.

"You were telling me about Pele," he reminded her with far more calm than he was feeling.

"Pele," Kara said without enthusiasm.

For a brief time, she had thought he was going to kiss her again, and even though she knew it was playing with fire, she couldn't resist the temptation to sample yet another one of those delicious kisses.

"Well," she continued after taking a deep breath, "Pele couldn't enjoy Lohiau while she was in spirit form. So she hurried back to her firepit and sent her sister Hiiaka to bring him back."

"Did Hiiaka share her sister's rather heated charms?"

"You're getting ahead of me," Kara complained. "Of course the plot thickened when Hiiaka fell in love with Lohiau herself. Pele, not being naive, suspected as much, and in revenge she caused Halemaumau to erupt. The climax came when Hiiaka returned with Lohiau and, in the midst of the volcanic eruption, made love to him on the edge of the firepit. And that's the painting you're going to have gracing your walls," she finished with a smile.

"That's fine with me."

Kara stopped in her tracks. "You've got to be kidding. It's one of the ugliest things Daddy's ever done."

Unable to resist for a moment longer, he dropped his shoes onto the sand and gathered her into his arms. "Ah, but whenever I look at it, I'll think of you."

In turn, Kara dropped her sandals on the beach and placed her hands on his shoulders. "Are you accusing sweet kind me of having a temper?"

His fingers stroked the fragile line of her cheekbones. "No," he murmured as he traced the exquisite planes and hollows of her face, "I'm accusing you of making things very, very warm around here."

She wound her arms around his neck. "Is that a complaint?" she asked on a soft, breathless voice.

"Never."

He was burning for her with a white-hot heat that infused his every pore. His hands, as they caressed her body, were not as steady as they should have been, and his mind was scorched with orange flames and fogged with a dark, dense smoke.

She brushed her lips against his, enticingly, tauntingly. His body shuddered; he could feel her satisfied smile against his lips.

"I love the way you kiss," she murmured. "Kiss me again, Adam. Kiss me now," she whispered heatedly.

Needing no further invitation, he thrust his hands into her hair, telling himself to go slowly, to savor the moment. But her eager lips were so hot and her hands, as they pulled his shirt loose to run desperately over his back, started new fires in him. His tongue entered the dark, secret interior of her mouth; she moaned and arched against him. His hands crushed the delicate fabric of her dress as they stroked her breasts, and as he felt the heat rising from her, Adam's own body burned in response.

They seemed to be standing on the very edge of Pele's furious volcano; flames tore at the fabric of their self-restraint, fire licked at their reason. Heat, fire, smoke surrounded them, threatening to sweep them into the fiery core. Slowly, gradually, Adam became aware of yet another sensation, the feel of soft, cool water against his heated skin.

"It's raining."

"Liquid sunshine," she corrected against his mouth. "Oh, more," she demanded, pressing her lips against his with renewed strength.

His body was still on fire, molten desire surged through his loins, and Adam knew that if he allowed this to continue, there would be no stopping things from taking their natural course.

Would that be so bad, he asked himself as her hands moved around to press against his chest, her fingers trailing a seductive path down his torso. What could be wrong with two people who were attracted to each other sharing a mutual desire? What indeed, he asked himself, even as he knew the answer. This siren, this fiery-haired Lorelei, was his best friend's sister.

There was another reason—one even more disconcerting, Adam admitted as the touch of her hands threatened to drive him over the edge. These sensations—the heat, the hunger, the need—were too threatening for a man used to being in control of every situation. He had the vague, uneasy feeling that if he wasn't careful, he could easily lose the ability to determine his own destiny.

"Kara," he warned, "we have to stop."

Her lips plucked at his, enticingly, wantonly. She was under the spell of the moonlight, the romantic scent of the frangipani, the seductive sea breeze. Kara couldn't remember ever feeling that way, and she wanted to continue to explore the thrilling new sensation.

A little while, she assured herself. *Just a little while longer. Then we'll stop*, she promised. *Just a little more.*

"Why?" she whispered. The sensual throb of the surf pounded in her veins.

"Because in another minute I'm going to forget I'm a gentleman."

She pressed her mouth against his throat, loving the musky scent that lingered on his skin. "Don't you ever give in to impulse?"

He threw back his head and laughed at that. "Sweetheart, what do you think I've been doing all day?"

His frank response broke the sensual mood. Something in his tone alerted her. "You don't sound as if you're very happy about it," she said, dropping her eyes to the coral sand and her hands to her sides.

Damn. He'd only wanted to save himself; he hadn't meant to hurt her. Putting a finger under her chin, he lifted her strangely wary gaze to his.

"I suppose I'm not," he admitted with a long, deep sigh. "Look, Kara," Adam tried to explain with a gentleness he had not known he possessed, "I've been under a lot of pressure lately. I came down here to try to figure out what I was doing with my life and where I was going."

"And where you'd gone wrong?" she asked quietly, unable to resist smoothing away the line etched between his brows.

She'd hit the bull's-eye. To everyone else, it looked as if Adam Lassiter should be riding on top of the world: a high position on an important commission, national press attention, invitations from both parties to run for political office. He was exactly where he had set out to be so many years ago. But why was he dissatisfied? The fact that Kara could have so easily recognized a feeling that he had kept carefully hidden hinted at a depth in her that he was honestly surprised to discover.

He managed a grim smile. "You didn't warn me that you had second sight."

She shrugged. "You never asked," she pointed out succinctly. "Besides, we've only just met today."

He eyed her thoughtfully. "We have rushed things a little, haven't we?"

Her skin gleamed like satin in the moonlight. Unable to resist touching her again, Adam ran his fingers over her shoulders. She trembled at the light caress.

"Sometimes," she answered slowly, carefully, "you have to go with your impulses. It's like being on top of the high dive and looking down that frighteningly long way to the pool. If you allow yourself to think about it, you'd climb right back down again. Sometimes you just have to close your eyes and dive in."

His brows drew together. "And what if you land in dangerous waters?" he asked, trailing his hand down her throat. Her pulse quickened under his lingering touch.

He would not be an easy man to know. Adam Lassiter operated on intellect and reason, while she preferred to allow her feelings to dominate her behavior. And right then her feelings were telling her that she was soon going to find herself over her head in those proverbial dangerous waters.

"That's the risk you take, I suppose."

He half smiled. "You make it sound so easy."

"And you make it sound so difficult."

They stared at each other, both searching for answers as the rain continued to fall. Finally Adam lifted a few heavy strands of wet hair off her face. Kara remained as still as a statue as he bent his head and his lips brushed her cheek.

"You taste like rain."

"Liquid sunshine," she corrected again as she closed her eyes to the exhilarating feel of his mouth on her skin. "It never rains in paradise, Adam. Didn't Colin tell you that when he was sending you down here to seduce me?"

He jerked his head up and glared down at her. "Dammit, for once and for all, Colin offered me the cottage so I could get some much-needed relaxation. He never even mentioned that it came equipped with a lunatic sister."

His words hurt more than she would have thought possible. Moments later, anger rose to wash over the pain. "That's not a very nice thing to say!"

God, she was magnificent, Adam decided, her head thrown back, her eyes shooting angry sparks, her hands splayed on the soft, inviting swell of her hips. It was all he could do not to toss her over his shoulder and take her back to Colin's crazily decorated seduction den.

"What else am I supposed to think about a grown woman who wishes on rainbows, has a dog the size of a Buick for a brother and talks to fish?" His eyes narrowed. "You can't expect me to believe that fish—Moby Dick, wasn't it—talks to you."

She tilted her chin slightly, daring him to say another derogatory word. "Are you accusing me of being a liar?"

"I'm accusing you," he said slowly, enunciating every word, "of having an imagination that makes your older brother look like a rank amateur. I'm accusing you of using your rather unique charms to drive me to distraction from the moment I met you.

"And—" he leaned down, his mouth a breath away from hers "—I'm accusing you, lady, of being a very dangerous, very delectable witch."

His eyes were dark and stormy with a spiraling need that Kara guessed was both unbidden and unwelcome. She wondered what Adam would say if she told him that she was feeling the very same way about him.

"A witch? It's obvious that you're not planning to seduce me with flattery and pretty compliments."

His lips drew into a tight, hard line. "I think you have it a little confused," he said gruffly. "Just who's seducing whom?"

"I don't know," she admitted quietly. "It seems to be a mutual effort; the only trouble is, we keep getting out of sync."

Her words echoed what he had been feeling from the beginning. Adam managed a crooked smile. "It's late," he said quietly. "And you're getting wet."

"So are you."

He glanced down, surprised to find his own clothing drenched. "So I am. But it looks better on you."

His slow, lingering gaze roved over Kara, and he enjoyed the way the wet material clung to her body in the moon-spangled darkness, teasing the eye, tormenting the senses.

"I do want you, you know," he said with a deep, strangely regretful sigh.

"I know," Kara murmured. Then she flashed him an unaffected smile that jolted him to the core. "We have a saying around here, Adam: 'The faster you go, the more you miss along the way.'"

Rising up on her bare toes, she brushed her lips tantalizingly against his. "You wouldn't want to miss anything, would you?"

She bent down, scooped up her sandals and went running up the beach toward her cottage. The Pacific trade winds carried her laughter to his ears even after she'd closed her door.

Picking up his own shoes, Adam strolled past the cottage, fighting the urge to march up those steps, break down the door and make love to her the way he wanted to. But that would be giving in to impulse, and it had been years since anyone had accused Adam Lassiter of being an impulsive man.

4

THE HARSH DEMAND of the phone jolted Adam from what had promised to be a very erotic and highly frustrating dream. He fumbled for the receiver without opening his eyes.

"What is it?" he barked.

"So much for Hawaii filling you with the old aloha spirit," the deep male voice said with a laugh.

"Aloha spirit be damned," Adam growled as he sat up in bed. "What the hell did you have in mind, anyway?"

"In mind?" Colin Tiernan repeated blankly. "Concerning what?"

Adam's scowling gaze circled the ridiculously seductive room. "Your redecorating, for one thing."

"How did it turn out?" Colin inquired interestedly.

"Like something out of an old movie: me Tarzan, you Jane. For God's sake, Colin, haven't you ever heard of overkill?"

"Sounds like Kara followed my instructions to a T."

Adam could hear the smile in his best friend's voice. "Speaking of your sister," he began, not bothering to hide his belief that Kara had been right about one thing: Colin had definitely set them up.

Colin's next words confirmed his suspicions. "Isn't she something? Face like a Botticelli angel, figure as sleek as a Thoroughbred and a spirit to match. Damn, if she wasn't my own flesh and blood, I'd probably fall for her myself."

Adam didn't bother to deny that he had responded precisely as predicted. "Nevertheless, that was dirty pool, my friend."

"Hell, Adam, you and Kara are my best friends. So I couldn't resist the temptation to meddle a little. What are you going to do, arrest me?"

"What are you going to do if I seduce your sister?"

"I suppose that depends on what your intentions are," Colin answered instantly. "Actually, now that you mention it, I was rather planning to have to go out and buy a wedding gift."

"I'm hardly in the market for a wife; in case you've forgotten, I'm supposed to be here on Kauai recharging for my appointment as chief of police."

It had been agreed that the news of his upcoming promotion, something he had worked long and hard for, would for the present be kept within an intimate circle of four—the mayor, the police commissioner, the current police chief, who was retiring next month, and Adam. The fact that he hadn't hesitated to reveal the secret to Colin was yet another proof of their close friendship.

"So you're actually going to accept the appointment."

Adam thought he detected a hint of censure in Colin's voice. "That's been the plan from the beginning."

"Not exactly the beginning," Colin was quick to point out. "I seem to remember an idealistic, wet-behind-the-ears rookie who kept spouting off about helping the little people, making the world a better place to live in, unimportant little things like that. If I recall correctly, you didn't get interested in climbing that old ladder of success until Marilyn came along."

"Marilyn had nothing to do with it," Adam countered irritably. One thing he didn't need that morning was a lecture about his former wife.

"Didn't she?"

"Not at all," Adam lied unconvincingly. "Besides, what makes you think I won't be in a better position to help the little people when I'm chief?"

"In the first place, you'll never even see the people you're supposed to be helping," Colin retorted. "Your world will consist solely of politicians and the press; you'll be even more isolated than you are now. . . .

"And," he added, "Kara would hate living in San Francisco almost as much as she'd hate playing the role of the police chief's wife."

"Colin, your sister was emphatic about the fact that she has no more desire to get married than I do. So why don't you do us both a big favor and butt out?"

There was a long, significant pause on the other end of the overseas line. Finally Adam heard Colin's slight sigh. "Okay, so maybe it was a little crazy—"

"Crazy?" Adam shouted his frustration into the mouthpiece. "Do you have any idea what you've done?"

Again that lingering silence. "That bad, huh?" Colin said finally.

"If she wasn't your sister, I wouldn't even be talking to you this morning, because I would have been far too occupied with more pleasurable pursuits to answer the phone."

"Marriage isn't such a bad institution, you know," Colin offered helpfully.

"Strange words from a man who isn't in the habit of allowing his women guests to spend the night."

"Women interfere with my work," Colin declared. "They demand too much time and attention and never seem to understand why I can't work on a strict nine-to-five schedule. On the other hand, Kara is precisely what you need right now. A lot more than you need another fool promotion."

"You've got a beautiful sister, Colin. She's also, in a strange, otherworldly way, sexy as hell. But—"

"Did you ever wonder why you've never remarried, Adam?" Colin cut in abruptly.

"I've never given a great deal of thought to the matter," Adam said dryly. "But I suppose you're going to tell me that you have."

"Of course I have; it's my job to delve under the surface of things."

"You write horror novels."

"So? Actually, I write stories about horrifying things happening to ordinary people, if you want to be specific. Anyway, the way I see it, the reason you've never really fallen in love is because you've dated a series of identical, proper, polite, predictable women. Admittedly, they're beautiful and intelligent, but they're all cut from the same cookie cutter. They are also unbelievably boring."

"Thank you for the lecture on my love life," Adam responded curtly. "Now, if you don't mind, I think I'll go back to sleep and for the sake of our friendship, I'll try to forget this conversation ever occurred."

"You do that," Colin Tiernan agreed in an obliging manner. "But, Adam—"

"What now?"

"You don't have to marry her if you don't really want to. But don't hurt her."

"One thing I don't need is a lecture from a man who had a revolving door installed in his house just to handle the number of women passing through," he shot back. "Dammit, Colin, Kara is a grown woman!"

"She's also a lot more vulnerable than she looks," Colin said seriously, hanging up before Adam could respond.

Frustrated, Adam slammed the receiver down with undue force, causing the bell to jangle. A moment later, he heard a light tapping at his door.

"Damn," he ground out. He wrapped the leopard fur around his waist, marched into the front room and threw open the screen door.

"Now what?" he demanded furiously.

Adam's irritation dissolved like a sandcastle under high tide as he viewed Kara, scantily clad in a bright pink bikini, looking as if she should be served up in a sugar cone. She was wearing a flowered shirt over the bikini, but hadn't bothered to button it. At the enticing sight of all that golden flesh, Adam recalled the erotic dream Colin had interrupted.

Kara didn't falter under Adam's blistering gaze. After lying awake all night considering the matter, she had decided that Adam Lassiter was in dire need of a strong dose of fun. And she was going to see that he learned to enjoy himself, whether he wanted to or not.

"Good morning," she said, brushing past him into the cottage. "I come bearing gifts." The heady scent of her tantalized his nostrils as she walked by.

Adam raked his hand through his hair, shaking his head as he followed her into the kitchen. "What kind of gifts?" he asked suspiciously.

She carried a small wicker basket, which she put on the table. "Coffee," she said with a smile, taking out a red thermos. "I didn't think you would have gone to the market yet. And bagels, with my own special spread."

He lifted a brow. "Eye of newt?"

Kara gave him a long, patient look. "I'll overlook that for the sake of neighborly friendship. But don't push me, Adam. Or you might get more than you bargained for."

"I already have," he grumbled. "Your brother called."

She had been in the process of taking a pair of plates down from the cupboard. At his words, she glanced back over her shoulder. "Of course you accused Colin of behaving unconscionably."

"Not in so many words, but I did tell him that we're capable of handling our own affairs."

She nodded in agreement as she put the plain white plates on the table beside the thermos. "Interesting choice of words," she murmured. "Is that what we're going to have? An affair?"

She turned back for the cups. As she reached up, her shirt rose, displaying a weakening amount of creamy hip. Adam swallowed.

"I'd say that's up to you. He also warned me that you're more vulnerable than you look."

To Adam's amazement, Kara slammed the earthenware mugs down beside the plates. "Damn him. He had no right!"

"Hey," he soothed, "he was just trying to play the big brother. It's not that big a deal."

Her soft eyes were swimming with tears that Kara refused to allow herself to shed. "What else did he tell you about me?"

There was something in her tone, barely perceptible, but there just the same, that rang a warning bell in Adam's mind. If he didn't know better, he'd think she was afraid. But of what? He had never met a more open, forthright individual. What secrets could Kara Tiernan possibly be hiding?

Deciding that his imagination was getting as active as the Tiernans', Adam shook off the odd premonition.

"He didn't tell me anything, Kara," he assured her quietly. Something flickered in her dark eyes that he would have sworn was panic. "Except to suggest that you're exactly what I need in a wife." That admission was accompanied by a broad smile that invited her to see the humor in their situation.

Kara was aware of what Adam was doing and appreciated it at the same time as she wondered if he could guess that her heart was beating wildly, out of control.

"Too bad you're not going to run for governor," she said, struggling to force her frozen lips into a smile. "I'd make a wonderful first lady; think of the fortune I could save the taxpayers by doing my own repairs to the executive mansion."

He brushed his knuckles down her cheek, marveling, not for the first time, at the satiny texture of her flawless skin. "Let's not overlook the kick the press would get out of the governor's bedroom," he suggested, getting into the swing of the fanciful game, hoping to relax her a bit. Adam would not have guessed she could be so tense: her slender body was rigid.

"Passion in paradise," she suggested softly, wanting to close her eyes at his tender touch, which seemed to be offering comfort rather than seduction.

"And we'd hang your father's painting over our bed." Adam toyed with a bright, fiery curl. "The one with Hiiaka and Lohiau making love on the edge of the volcano."

The uncharacteristic moisture in her eyes disappeared, replaced by a slow, simmering warmth. "No," she murmured, struggling to keep her mind on their foolish banter as he drew her nearer, just by tugging lightly on her hair.

"No?" He wrapped a long strand around his hand. "Are you telling me we're not going to have an original Michael Tiernan gracing our bedchamber? What will Californian art critics say?"

"Since you're so enamored of my father's work, I thought you could hang it in your office."

"In my office?" Adam feigned horrified shock at the suggestion. "Out in the open? Where all my visitors can see it?"

"In your office," she repeated firmly. "I'd love to watch you trying to explain that it's only your aesthetic sense that's clouded, not your judgment."

Kara patted his cheek comfortingly, enjoying the rough male texture of his unshaven skin against her palm. "Just be grateful that you're not running for office," she said. "And that neither one of us wants to get married."

The laughter he was used to hearing in her voice was back, and Adam felt as if the sun had just come from behind a dark cloud to brighten his day.

"Lucky thing."

"Isn't it?" she agreed.

"Speaking of marriage, how's your friend?"

Kara's smooth brow furrowed. "I don't really know. I tried to call her last night from my parents'. And again after I got home. And three times this morning." She shook her head. "But there wasn't any answer."

"Maybe she and this Brett guy eloped last night," he suggested. "Perhaps that's what she was calling to tell you."

"Perhaps," Kara murmured, clearly unconvinced. "Oh, well, I'll find out soon enough, I suppose. I'm going to keep trying to get hold of her today. Brett runs a charter boat; I thought it would be fun if we could all have a twilight dinner sail this evening.

"Do you want your coffee now? Or after your shower?" Kara asked briskly as she bustled around the kitchen as if it were her own.

"I'll take a shower first," he decided. *A cold one*, he tacked on mentally as he left the room before he said the hell with breakfast and settled for dessert, instead.

"I WAS GOING to replace your bathroom tile today," Kara announced as Adam returned to the kitchen. "But I changed my mind."

She glanced up at him, deciding that the lightweight khaki slacks and blue, button-down oxford cloth shirt were an improvement of sorts. The tasseled loafers, however, were going to have to go.

"Please tell me Colin didn't choose black marble," he asked hopefully, taking the mug she handed him with a smile of appreciation.

She laughed at that. "No, he didn't go that far, thank God. Actually, it's a very nice, very subdued ivory. I think you'll like it. When I get around to installing it, that is."

The kitchen wall was almost entirely made of glass, allowing a breathtaking view of clear water in many shades of blue, edged by a dazzling white crescent of sand. Taking in the idyllic scene, Adam began to understand what Kara had meant when she said that the islands invited a person to slow down and enjoy life.

"So what's on the agenda?" Taking a drink of the rich black coffee, he watched Kara dump two heaping spoonfuls of sugar into hers, taste, then add one more for good measure. "That's disgusting."

"Isn't it?" she agreed cheerfully. "My dentist agrees with you, of course, despite the fact that I've never had a cavity in my life. To answer your question, I've got the day all planned. First, we're taking you shopping."

He put his mug down on the table and folded his arms across his chest. "I am not, under any circumstances, going to wear one of those damned flowered shirts."

Kara reminded herself to be patient. He was, after all, a *malihini*—a newcomer—and should be allowed time to adjust. "Tom Selleck wears them," she coaxed prettily.

"Selleck is an actor," he replied, his acid tone indicating his prejudices concerning that particular profession. "He's *expected* to be flamboyant. It's all part of his image."

"But not part of yours," she guessed.

He looked utterly horrified by the suggestion. "Kara, I'm a police captain! I'm supposed to be a symbol of authority."

Kara decided that this was not the time to point out that she wasn't any more fond of authority figures than she was of politicians.

"In California," she said instead, "where everyone's a little quirky. I happen to know for a fact that it's a state requirement; all newcomers are screened at the border for the Q.Q."

"Q.Q.?"

"Quirky Quotient."

He eyed the breakfast she had delivered with obvious suspicion. "Speaking of quirky, whoever heard of putting peanut butter and orange marmalade on a bagel?"

She waved away his complaint with a flick of her wrist. "It's good for you. I'll have you know that there are probably enough proteins and assorted minerals and vitamins in this breakfast to fulfill your minimum daily requirements until at least 1990.

"As for the shirt, I'll let you off the hook for now. But we're obviously going to have to get you some decent footwear."

He looked down at his calfskin loafers. "What's wrong with these?"

"They're beautiful, expensive and totally wrong for the beach."

"Who said anything about a beach? I'd planned to sit out on the terrace and get some work done today."

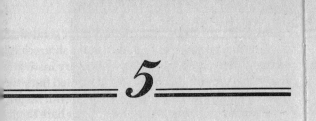

5

R IS ONE of Kauai's major industries," Kara said as she
l the fire-engine-red Jeep through the forest of tas-
ugarcane.

all her talk of the pleasures of life in the slow lane,
estimated that she was going at least sixty miles an
own the dirt road.

e other is the military; the navy has a base at Barking
"

shifted gears and pressed down on the accelerator,
g an enormous truck loaded with freshly cut sugar-
n the right. Adam resisted the impulse to close his

ually," she said, waving gaily at the truck driver she
st leaving behind in a cloud of dust, "sugar's so de-
ole that it's almost a religion on the island."

m glanced over at the speedometer. "Do you realize
st you're going?"

glanced down at the dashboard, switching gears
is the sugarcane became a blur. "I always drive more
on dirt roads."

n't wait until we get to the highway," he said dryly.

downshifted as she negotiated a tight turn, then
her foot down on the accelerator. "We'll be there in
te," she promised him with a smile.

n she came to a shuddering stop at the intersection,
s palms were braced against the dashboard. "Why
ou let me drive," he suggested hopefully.

"Wrong again," she answered cheerfully, ignoring his
threatening frown. "Today we're going sightseeing. And, if
you're very, very nice, I'll even introduce you to Moby
Dick."

"The talking fish," he muttered.

"The very same."

He shook his head. "I don't know which one of us is
crazier—you for talking to a fish, or me for agreeing to tag
along to watch you do it."

Kara had only a split second to decide whether to be annoyed or amused by his aggrieved tone. She opted for
amusement.

"Don't knock it," she said with a jaunty grin, "until you've
tried it. You know, Adam, it certainly wouldn't hurt if you
allowed yourself a little fantasy now and then."

She got up from the table, intending to take her mug to
the sink to wash it out, but Adam caught hold of her wrist.
"What makes you think I don't entertain any fantasies?"

His voice was husky, thickened with barely restrained
hunger, and his eyes, as they locked on to hers, were like a
tempest-tossed sea. Slowly, deliberately, Kara forced herself to relax.

"I was simply teasing, Adam. Gracious, must you take
everything so seriously?"

He'd told himself during that long and icy shower that he
wouldn't touch her, yet he found himself pulling her down
onto his lap. Unable to resist the enticing scent emanating
from her skin, he pressed his lips against her temple.

"I'm a serious person, Kara. I always have been."

The fact that he had said it so simply, without apology,
made Kara stifle her sigh. With a fingertip, she traced his
smoothly shaven jawline, breathing in the crisp scent of his
soap.

"I'll bet you were a Boy Scout."

"Eagle," he admitted.

She smiled at that. "Why aren't I surprised?"

Adam ran his palm over her hair. "I wouldn't think anything could ever surprise you."

What should have been a casual touch made her tremble. As she sought to understand what Adam was doing to her, Kara realized that it was because for him there were no casual touches. No simple conversations. Everything he did, every word that escaped those firm lips, was gravely serious, meticulously planned.

A part of her grieved for the young man she had not appreciated when they'd first met: the rookie patrolman who had acted on his instincts. Instincts that were undeniably dangerous, perhaps even a bit foolish. That young man probably would not have risen through the ranks as far as the one now sitting with her in Colin's sunny kitchen. But she'd bet her new titanium diver's watch with electronic depth meter that he would have gotten a lot more fun out of life.

Oh, Colin, she thought, *even if I had been wanting to fall in love, you couldn't have sent me a more unlikely candidate.*

Kara's wide gray eyes, as they met his, were full of undisguised emotion. "You've surprised me, Adam," she said quietly. "More than I would have thought possible."

Instead of looking pleased by her admission, Adam frowned. "Kara—"

No, Kara reflected, nothing about Adam Lassiter was going to be easy. Again, she forced herself to relax.

"We're losing the day," she said with forced brightness, pressing a quick, hard, almost desperate kiss against his tight lips. "Come on, Captain, I'm going to get you to unwind if it's the last thing I do."

The hell with Colin and the hell wit[h] [be]havior, Adam decided as he looked at the woman. He wanted her. And unless eve[ry] [he pos]sessed had gone on the blink, Kara war[ted him.] hadn't she told him he should learn to g[o]

He ran a slow, insinuating hand up he[r] think of better ways to relax than runn[ing] tourist all day."

She slid off his lap in a smooth, deft you go again, city man. Rushing things. at him. "Didn't anyone ever tell you th[at] half the fun?"

With that she headed toward the doo[r] over her shoulder. "Are you coming o[r]

Shaking his head with mute frustrati[on] the chair, grabbing his camera from w[here] terday on the counter.

"Coming," he grumbled, wonderin[g] had let himself in for.

She looked in both directions, engaged the clutch, shifted into first and took off with a roar that forced Adam back in his seat. "Because you don't know where you're going," she answered patiently. "Sit back and enjoy yourself, Adam, while I play tour guide."

He had never thought of himself as cowardly, but as she swerved to avoid a long-legged white bird that had suddenly darted onto the road, Adam closed his eyes, willing his heart to keep beating.

"Do you think we could take this tour at a pace somewhat less than the speed of sound?"

She looked somewhat surprised by his ironic tone, but eased up on the accelerator. "That's the Sleeping Giant." She pointed toward a rock formation that did indeed resemble a reclining Goliath. "He was the giant Puni, who befriended the Menehune.

"Little people," she explained at his questioning look. "They were here even before the first Hawaiians arrived. They were two feet tall and did all their work at night. They also had magical powers."

"I suppose you believe in them," Adam responded, venturing a guess.

Kara turned her head to give him a knowing grin. "I like to," she admitted, "although there are those horribly unromantic souls who persist in believing that the Menehune were actually a class of pygmy laborers from Tahiti."

"You have to admit it makes more sense than the idea of pixies."

Apparently Kara was not prepared to concede any such point. "To some. However, while historians and anthropologists continue to argue about the Menehune, no one has come up with a logical explanation for all the stone water projects that were supposedly built by the Menehune in a single night.

"Anyway," she continued, "one time Puni was asleep when enemy canoes were threatening to beach on the shoreline. The Menehune threw boulders onto his stomach to wake him up so he could come and protect them, but he was snoring and swallowed some of the boulders and died."

He had to fight the smile that threatened to appear at the sight of Kara's serious face. "That's too bad."

"Isn't it," she agreed with a slight sigh. "Still, a few rocks ricocheted off his belly and sank the invaders' canoes, so it all worked out in the end, I suppose."

She belonged here, Adam determined. In fact, he had never met an individual more suited to her environment. Cinderella, Sleeping Beauty, King Arthur, all would feel at home in this fantasy land of nature and legend. Adam was having difficulty picturing Kara living anywhere else.

"That's Anahola Beach," she said, waving her right hand in the direction of a quiet stretch of sand they were passing. "The water's calm there; it's ideal for swimming."

She downshifted, slowing the Jeep to allow Adam a leisurely look at the glistening beach. "Of course Kauai is one of the greatest places in the world for beaches," she continued. "It's because we're the oldest island in the Hawaiian chain, so nature has had more time to create our gorgeous beaches.

"Kalapaki Beach is great for windsurfing, Polpu Beach and Brenneck's Beach are good for bodysurfing, windsurfing and catamaran rides. Shipwreck Beach is where you'll find a lot of swimmers, and Pakala Beach is good for surfing—"

"I get the point," he broke in. "And it's nice of you to play tour guide, Kara, but I don't really think I'll have time for surfing and catamaran rides. I do have—"

"Work to do," she said, cutting him off, just as he had interrupted her.

Adam thought he detected the hint of an accusation in her dry tone. "That's right. I've got stacks of commission papers to go through, files filled with data to digest—"

"So why did you come down here?" she asked, genuinely curious. "Surely you could have gone over your precious papers in San Francisco as well as on Kauai."

"Of course I could have. But I wanted a change."

"Of pace? Or location?"

"Is there a difference?"

As they continued down the highway, the scenic bay curved out toward the backdrop of mountains. Rainwater scored the lush green mountain face in rivulets of molten silver. Adam tried to remember when he had seen anything so magnificent.

"It depends," Kara answered at length. "If you lock yourself away in Colin's house and do nothing but pore over those papers, then you might as well have stayed home; a change in location isn't going to matter.

"However, if you forget about your work for a while and open yourself up to everything Kauai has to offer, then I'd say you did the right thing coming here."

"And what, exactly, does Kauai have to offer?"

Kara would have had to be deaf or an idiot to miss the sensual implication in Adam's deep voice. "The best way to find that out," she said, decelerating as she suddenly turned off the main highway, "is to take things one day at a time and leave yourself open to surprises."

Adam didn't respond, but he couldn't help wondering if Kara realized that she was the most disturbing surprise he had had in years. In a lifetime, he amended, casting a quick, sidelong glance at her profile.

The short road cut through the lush, fragrant greenery, ending at a tall white lighthouse.

"Kilauea lighthouse," Kara announced in her tour-guide voice as she brought the Jeep to a sudden stop with a screech of brakes. "The lighthouse, standing on the northernmost point of Kauai, serves as a beacon to ships and planes en route to and from the Orient. It also claims the largest clamshell lens in existence. These days the lighthouse is fully automated, but as you'll see, the view is spectacular."

"It is certainly that," Adam agreed, his eyes on Kara as she jumped out of the Jeep. The shirt fell midway to her thighs, drawing attention to her smooth, golden-tanned legs.

"This is also the largest bird-nesting area in the Hawaiian chain. The birds you see are the red-footed booby and the black-footed albatross, better known as the gooney."

The urge to touch her was suddenly overwhelming. Adam reached out and brushed his thumb along her cheekbone. "All these years that he's extolled your many virtues, Colin forgot to mention what an attractive woman you are."

"You know how brothers are," she said lightly. "Colin undoubtedly still thinks of me as having red braids down to my waist—which he yanked more times than I'd care to count, by the way—a hot temper and a mouth full of railroad tracks."

She flashed him a confident grin that was more than a little forced. If she had to tell the truth, Kara would have to admit to suddenly feeling incredibly uneasy. He was looking at her, his expression half desirous, half strangely irritated, and she didn't know which disturbed her more.

"Come see." Taking his hand, she led him to the edge of the bluff.

Multihued blue water swirled dizzyingly far below them, breaking on the rocks in sprays of frothy white sea foam. Quickly, unhesitatingly, with the air of a man who knows exactly what he wants and doesn't believe in wasting time vacillating over viewpoints, Adam lifted his camera and froze the scene on thirty-five-millimeter film.

Kara was standing on a rock beside him. Her eyes, bright with exhilaration, were level with his. "Isn't it wonderful?" she asked breathlessly, throwing back her head to gaze out over the water, which reflected every color of blue from shimmering turquoise to deep indigo and all the shades in between.

"Every time I come here, I have an almost uncontrollable urge to fling open my arms and fly off into the wild blue yonder, like Jonathan Livingston Seagull." Her lips curved into a wide smile. "Some kids dream of digging to China. I always wanted to fly there."

Her cheeks were flushed a deep apricot, her eyes as silver as whitecaps glistening under a full moon. Her sun-drenched hair was blowing free in the warm breeze, like a gilt-and-copper halo. She looked every bit as carefree, as welcoming, as the native Hawaiian women must have looked, standing on this very bluff, watching Captain Cook's ships sail up the coast.

No wonder the seamen fell in love with the islands, Adam mused. Kara Tiernan was part fantasy, part flesh-and-blood woman. And he wanted both more than he could remember wanting anything in his life.

He was struck by a sudden urge to capture the breath-takingly beautiful sight of her on film. Years from now, when he was worrying about rising crime statistics, over-crowded prisons or whatever other problems the future might bring, he could drag out this photograph and remember what total freedom looked like.

"Really, Adam," Kara complained lightly when she heard the unmistakable sound of a shutter release, "if I'd known you were in the market for a model, I would have brought along one of my father's."

"I don't want one of your father's models. I want you."

There was a hint of annoyance in his tone, one Kara decided to ignore. She turned back toward the Jeep. "We need to get back on the highway. I still have a lot to show you."

Reaching across the space between them, Adam ran his fingers down the back of her neck. "I thought that 'the smiles you collect along the way are more important than the miles covered.'"

In spite of the pounding in her veins, she managed a smile at the familiar Hawaiian saying. "You're catching on, Captain Lassiter. There may just be hope for you yet."

"I certainly hope so," he murmured huskily as he leaned down to kiss her.

His lips were firm, their purposeful assault as decisive as the man himself. Yet rather than demanding a response, they coaxed silkily, enticing her to join in the slow, serious kiss.

The breeze cooling her uplifted face was tinged with the crisp, tangy scent of the sea and the sun felt warm, blissfully so, against her eyelids. Below, she could hear the crash of the surf as it beat endlessly against the rocks, and somewhere in the distance a seabird called out as it scanned the surging tide for silvery fish.

The reality of place and time gradually ebbed, and Kara clung to Adam's shoulders as she seemed to feel the ground giving way beneath her feet, like sands under a retreating wave.

When her mouth opened in a soft sigh of acceptance and wonder, Adam easily slipped his tongue between her lips, and suddenly the kiss, which had begun like so many others, was strangely, overwhelmingly different. She was caught up in a wildness beyond anything she had ever known, swept away by feelings that were even older than the forces that had formed the cliff on which they stood.

Responding fully to the kiss, Kara lifted her arms, linking them around his neck. The gesture fitted her slender curves more tightly against him, making Adam's body ache with anticipation. His fingers tangled in her hair, holding her face still as he deepened the kiss, urging her further and further into the storm.

"Let's go back to the cottage," he groaned against her lips.

She trembled as his hands moved up and down her back under the cotton shirt, turning her skin to flame. "But the tour—"

"Damn the tour," he muttered, clutching her hips and pulling her against him. "I want you, Kara. And I want you now."

Frustration and his conflicting feelings for Kara brought an unmistakably masculine insistence to his words. Kara felt herself slowly, reluctantly, coming back to earth.

"Do you always get what you want?" she asked quietly, tilting her head back to look up at him. A dangerous storm still swirled in his cobalt eyes.

He was losing it; Adam could feel the moment disappearing like sand sifting through open fingers. He fought against the unreasonable urge to throw her onto the soft bed of brilliant flowers beneath their feet and take her there. Now. He knew that in her heart, it was what Kara wanted, as well. He couldn't be the only one experiencing these unruly feelings of desire.

"Yes." There was a challenge in his gritty tone.

Kara wondered fleetingly what it was like to know that you had the world at your fingertips, that whatever you could ever want was within reach. A moment later, she decided that though she was as attracted to Adam as he appeared to be to her, she was not going to become simply another one of his easy victories.

"Then this afternoon should come as a refreshing change of pace," she replied blithely. Stepping out of his embrace, she continued walking toward the Jeep.

Adam caught up with her. "Dammit, I don't want a change of pace. I want you."

She had control again—no small feat—and now, when she risked a glance upward, her gaze was serene. "I heard you the first time, Adam," she said quietly.

Not knowing how to respond, he refrained from answering for a long, silent interlude. From time to time, as she drove along the coast, Kara would sneak a glance at him as she pointed out different scenic attractions, but from the granite set of his jaw, she could only conclude that he intended to sulk for the remainder of the afternoon.

Men, she mused exasperatedly. They were so damnably sensitive—why did women bother to put up with them at all? As soon as Kara had asked herself that rhetorical question, the memory of the way Adam's kisses made her body glow like molten lava provided the definitive answer.

"Here we are," Kara said as she pulled the Jeep off the road several minutes later. She glanced over at his stony face. "Just as a matter of idle curiosity, are you going to sulk all day?"

Adam directed his gaze out over the seemingly endless expanse of turquoise water. "I'm certainly not sulking."

Kara ran her fingers over the top of the steering wheel. "Aren't you?"

He spun around, fixing her with a hard glare. He couldn't remember a time when he had felt more frustrated or powerless. Adam knew he wasn't alone in his feelings; Kara could never have feigned the passion that was starkly evident whenever he kissed her. Touched her. So why was she insisting on baiting him like this, offering herself, then dancing out of reach? It didn't make sense. Unless—

"Tell me something," he demanded suddenly.

She nodded. "If I can."

"You're not one of those women who get their kicks driving men to icy showers, are you?"

A slight smile made the corners of her mouth tilt upward. "What do you think?" she countered evenly.

His dark eyes moved over her sun-kissed face. "You're not," he decided after a lengthy pause. "So why are you doing this to me?"

Kara exhaled a small sigh. "To us," she corrected. Her tone was soft, unmistakably regretful, but firm nevertheless. "This isn't any easier on me, Adam. I think I've wanted to make love with you since the first moment I saw you staggering up the beach, loaded down with that computer and all those suitcases full of books and commission papers."

Despite her less than flattering description, Adam wasn't particularly surprised that she'd felt that same jolt of physical attraction. What was a revelation, however, was the way she stated her feelings so openly and honestly. Most women of his acquaintance—hell, Adam amended, all of them—would have been much more circumspect.

"Then why—"

She reached out, pressing her fingertips against his lips. "Things are different for you. You live in the city; you're sophisticated, used to having casual affairs. Your Rolodex is probably filled with the names of hundreds of beautiful, chic women you've made love with."

Adam had to bite back the smile her earnest expression and exaggerated idea of his sex life invited. "You make it sound as if I live in Sodom instead of San Francisco."

"Are you laughing at me?"

He shook his head. Although he was as frustrated as ever, his irritation had evaporated. "No, I'm just intrigued by your idea of my decadent life-style. If you were anywhere near the mark, I wouldn't have the energy to get out of bed in the morning, let alone put in an eighteen-hour work-day."

Color rose in her cheeks, and she managed an answering smile. "Touché. But the fact remains that San Francisco, though admittedly not Sodom, is still a long way from Kauai. Everyone knows everyone on the island; that tends to make one more discreet."

He reached out, trailing his fingers up the slanted line of her cheekbone where moments before roses had bloomed so appealingly.

"Are you saying that you're worried about your reputation?" he asked, still not quite understanding her meaning. From what he had witnessed thus far, none of the members of the Tiernan family would be likely to allow anyone to dictate their behavior.

The heat created by his caressing fingertips as they skimmed over her face threatened to prove her undoing. Kara leaned against the door of the Jeep, moving out of range of Adam's enticing touch. She tilted her head, studying him thoughtfully.

"I'm getting a little tired of having to justify not falling into bed with you at first sight," she complained mildly. "We don't even know each other."

He twined a fiery curl around his finger. "Can you think of a better way to get acquainted?"

Kara forced herself to be very still. His rich voice was beguiling, his blue eyes coaxed acquiescence and, against every bit of common sense, Kara's body yearned for him. The idea that he could create such turmoil in her with so little effort was distinctly frightening. And annoying.

"I think," she said slowly, carefully, "that you're pushing your luck."

"I've always been a very lucky man," he murmured, resting his hands on her shoulders. His fingers caressed her collarbone. "You're an exciting woman, Kara. I can't remember when I've wanted anyone as much as I want you."

His dark brooding eyes dropped to her mouth. "We're going to make love, sooner or later. Though I'm discovering that I'm a very impatient man, I'm willing to grant you the right to choose the time. But the outcome is inevitable, Kara."

Kara gathered her forces of resistance even as her need for him battered her. She tossed back her hair. "Watch it, Captain," she advised dryly. "Your ego is showing."

"So sue me," he murmured, lowering his head to hers, his intent obvious.

Kara deftly ducked, sliding out of the Jeep before his lips could meet hers. "Moby Dick is waiting for his breakfast," she said in a calm voice that took every bit of her inner strength to maintain. "Are you coming or not?"

As she shrugged out of the colorful shirt, revealing a body that caused his to flame with instant response, Adam fought a surge of annoyance. Paradise, he decided with a reluctant sigh, was undoubtedly worth waiting for.

She had unearthed a pile of snorkeling equipment from the back of the Jeep and Adam managed a tight-lipped smile as he took a set of fins, snorkel and mask from her arms. "I wouldn't miss it for the world."

Kara gave him a suspicious look, then, shrugging lightly, she decided to pay no attention to the veiled sarcasm and headed toward the inviting blue water. Ignoring Adam entirely, she threw a towel down onto the sand, tugged on her mask, adjusted the strap and waded out into the warm water. When she had gone a few steps, she pulled on the black flippers and began swimming toward an outcropping of rocks. Adam followed without hesitation.

The pristine water, intricately laced with a network of coral formations, was teeming with marine life of all kinds. Sea grass waved serenely in the slight current while brilliantly colored and patterned fish dashed among the branches of coral like tropical birds flitting through the delicate limbs of stony trees.

Vivid pink and red sea anemones expanded like soft and brilliant flowers, their sinuous tentacles waving enticingly as they lured unsuspecting victims into their embrace. Black-banded triggerfish approached Adam curiously, searching for handouts, while a conspicuously striped orange-and-blue clownfish nestled safely among the stinging tentacles of a cluster of anemones.

A spiny lobster, looking like a giant insect, approached along the sandy bottom, armored legs lifted as if in protection. When the crustacean appeared as interested in this intruder in his underwater world as Adam was in him, Adam couldn't help wondering what the reaction would be if some creature twenty times human size walked down Market Street in San Francisco. Would people hold their ground, the way this crustacean was doing? He seriously doubted it.

Kara tapped him on the shoulder, interrupting his fanciful thoughts, as she pointed across the silent lagoon. Cruising toward them and ignoring the other fish with regal dignity was a large, blue, silver, and orange-speckled parrot fish. Schools of smaller fish obediently parted like a silver curtain as the parrot fish swam in an unwavering line toward Kara. In this underwater world, he was undeniably king.

Kara reached into a small bag, taking out a yellow high-impact plastic waterproof camera, which she handed to

Adam with a smile. Her eyes laughed behind the mask as the two-foot-long parrot fish nudged her insistently. Impatiently. While Adam used up a roll of film, the rainbow-hued parrot fish plucked frozen green peas from Kara's outstretched hand with comical but precise bucktoothed jaws, never once grazing her skin.

When Kara pointed toward Adam, appearing to introduce man and fish, Moby Dick's shiny black eyes seemed to meet Adam's in an almost human, oddly somber gaze. Then he blinked, giving Adam the strange impression that perhaps, just maybe, something had registered on both sides. Before Adam could dwell on the meaning of their silent exchange, a school of long-nose butterfly fish swam between them like a sunburst, shattering the fanciful interlude. Shaking his head bemusedly, he followed Kara as she swam back toward the beach.

"Well," she demanded, pushing her mask up onto her forehead as they stood in the knee-deep water, "now you've met Moby Dick."

Adam took off his own mask. "So I have. But he didn't talk to me."

Kara shrugged. "Didn't I mention he uses telepathy?" she asked vaguely. Her teasing gaze turned suddenly serious. "What did you really think?"

He reached out, pushing back some clinging strands of wet hair from her face. "I think," he answered slowly, "that this morning will go down as one of the most overwhelmingly beautiful experiences of my life. Thank you for it."

His grave tone surprised her. "We were only snorkeling, Adam, something I do nearly every day. It's really not all that profound."

He pondered that for a moment. "Perhaps not profound," he agreed, "but vastly enjoyable. There was something almost—" he paused, as if searching for the proper word "—otherworldly about it."

Even as she experienced a rush of pleasure at his words, Kara was distressed by the fact that he had echoed her own thoughts so clearly. She had already decided to concentrate on all the things she and Adam Lassiter did not have in common. She preferred not to have to face the fact that they could possibly share anything besides physical attraction.

"You don't take much time out for enjoyment, do you, Adam?" she asked, forcing herself to focus once again on the differences between them.

"I've been known to play a hole or two of golf."

Her eyes narrowed against the sun as she looked up at him. "With the mayor and the police commissioner," she guessed correctly. "I'll bet you've never gotten through a game without discussing your work. You know your lowest score on every course you've ever played, and unless you at least match it every time out, you spend the remainder of the day irritated by your lousy performance."

He threw back his head and laughed. "I knew you were a witch. What do you do—spend your spare time peering into your crystal ball, spying on us poor mortals?"

She pressed her mouth against his in a firm, smacking kiss. "Now you're getting the idea, Captain."

When he would have wrapped his arms around her to hold her for a proper kiss, Kara backed away. "I don't know about you, but I'm starving," she said, running toward the Jeep.

Adam swore softly, as he admired the view of Kara from the rear. He was still standing in the water, forcing down his frustration, when the single cloud in the sky suddenly opened up, sending down a curtain of silvery rain.

"More liquid sunshine?" he asked as he helped Kara put the canvas top up on the Jeep.

She stuck out her tongue, tilting her head upward. "Uh-uh. Pineapple juice," she decided, fastening the top with a decisive snap.

He watched as she tugged a T-shirt over her head. The front was emblazoned with a brilliant silk-screened rainbow, not unlike the one they'd seen together last night.

"I just thought of a wish," he murmured, framing her in the lens of his camera and shooting.

She stopped in the process of tugging on a pair of white cotton shorts. "A wish?"

Following his wicked gaze, Kara glanced down at her chest. "Oh. That doesn't count; it has to be a real rainbow."

"Since when are you such a stickler for rules?"

Her grin was quick and filled with sunshine, denying the drops running down the windshield in silvery streaks. "Since I had to start dealing with you."

She tossed him his clothing. "Get dressed, Adam. I'm taking you to lunch."

She turned the key in the ignition and, with a roar of the four-cylinder engine, they headed back to the highway.

6

IN LESS THAN five minutes, Adam found himself seated at a tapa-topped lacquered table, facing a wall of glass that provided a panoramic view of Hanalei Bay.

When Kara had first led him up past the tiki poles that marked the entrance to the elegant restaurant, Adam had been struck by a sudden urge to put on a tie, despite the fact that his open-necked shirt and casual slacks were more formal than the attire of the majority of diners.

"Still suffering from cultural shock?" Kara asked sympathetically as she stirred her drink. A small paper parasol adorned the top of the red plastic swizzle stick.

He grimaced. "Is it that obvious?"

Kara observed him judiciously as she took a sip of the rum punch. "Only when you keep trying to straighten your tie," she decided.

Annoyed by the laughter in her eyes, Adam directed his attention toward the saltwater aquarium across the dining room. He was not used to being laughed at, particularly by a woman.

"I'm relieved to know that at least I'm providing some amusement," he said stiffly.

With a toss of her head, Kara speared a plump shrimp with a pair of bamboo chopsticks. "I don't recall your being so terribly sensitive."

His eyes narrowed. "I'm not sensitive."

"You could have fooled me. And when did they pass a law in San Francisco that says it's against the law for a police captain to have a sense of humor?"

"Are you aware that every time you refer to my occupation, you heap an extra helping of sarcasm on it?"

"Now who's got an overworked imagination? Are you going to eat your tempura or not?"

He cast a measuring eye over her slender frame, wondering where she put the food: she had the appetite of a truck driver and the body of a ballerina. Kara Tiernan was a constant study in contradictions. Although he refused to consider himself guilty of stereotyping, Adam had always felt more comfortable when he could put workable labels on individuals. So far, no matter how hard he tried, Kara was impossible to pigeonhole.

"Help yourself," he offered.

She flashed him a grin. "I love *mahimahi* this way," she said, plucking the fish from a thick black-bean sauce.

Adam leaned back in the bamboo chair and took a drink of the amber Scotch whiskey he'd ordered, ignoring Kara's protestations and the waiter's silent condemnation.

"When in Rome," Kara had told him yesterday. Well, that might be acceptable when it came to foregoing a necktie, but no one, not even the lovely and appealing Kara Tiernan, would persuade him to give up his Scotch for one of those frothy pastel concoctions that passed for drinks here on the island.

"You're ducking the question. What do you have against my work?"

"You're taking this far too personally, Adam."

"No, I don't think I am."

Her frustrated sigh ruffled her strawberry bangs. "For heaven's sake, it's not that I've actually got anything specific against your work—"

"You have no idea how that relieves my mind," he drawled.

"Do you want me to answer your question or not?"

He shrugged. "I'm probably going to regret this, but go ahead."

"I don't think you're happy."

"That's ridiculous. For your information, I've spent the past fifteen years working to get exactly where I am; I couldn't be happier."

She braced her elbows on the table, linking her fingers together. "If that's the case, then what are you doing here?"

"All right, I'll admit things have been hectic lately; I've been a little tense. Colin suggested I needed to unwind."

"I think you need more than that, Adam," Kara argued. "If you ask me, you've got all the symptoms of burnout."

"In the first place, you're dead wrong," he countered brusquely. "And in the second place, who are you to diagnose a case of occupational burnout? No offense, Kara, but you're not exactly the most hard-driving person I've ever met."

"I didn't think you'd listen," she said as she sat back in her chair and crossed her legs in a smooth movement that Adam couldn't help noticing despite his irritation. "But it was worth a try."

Her clear gray eyes met his in a long, level look. "Can you honestly tell me that you enjoy your work?"

"If it was supposed to be fun, they probably wouldn't call it work."

She shrugged, shifting her gaze to the magical vista of Hanalei Bay and the lush green mountains ablaze with flowers. "I can remember when you loved being a policeman," she said quietly.

"You were so busy complaining about everything and everyone around you that Christmas that I hadn't realized you'd noticed."

She gave him an enigmatic smile. "Oh, I noticed all right," she said softly. "Thinking back on it, I've come to the conclusion that part of the reason I behaved so abominably toward you was because of the way you made me feel."

As she reached for her glass again, Adam caught her hand in his. "What do you mean by that? Are you actually saying—"

"That you had a way of making me feel things I was too young to understand," she admitted in a soft rush of words.

Adam brushed his thumb over her wrist. Her pulse was fast. But steady. "And now?"

"I understand them all too well," she said with a light laugh as she slipped her hand from his. Her smile faded as she gave him a considering look. "Doesn't it get tiring?"

He leaned closer, idly playing with a lock of her hair. The silky curl carried the provocative scent of gardenias. "Doesn't what get tiring?"

"Always having to maintain a pose of being totally in control. Of continually being the man in charge."

"I'm used to it," he said simply.

Of course he was, Kara realized. As head of the commission, Adam had an image—in a state that thrived on image—of a paradoxical man who could be both charming and ruthless, intelligent and brusque. According to the *Time* article she had read, Adam had brought to his current job the same maze of contradictions that had baffled San Franciscans for some years. The fact that he was personally beguiling and politically enigmatic had only increased the public's interest.

"That's right," she murmured. "For a mere police captain, you have a public profile that's every bit as high as Johnny Carson's. Or Tom Cruise's."

"I'm not going to apologize for using the media, Kara. I always considered news coverage the best way to telegraph the message to crooks that society will not accept their actions. I hope that some of them will think twice before committing a crime."

Kara recalled a recent nationally aired interview. The toughness Adam Lassiter had projected when announcing the cracking of a ring that had made over four billion dollars in illegal profits by selling arms and aircraft to enemy governments had certainly dispelled any idea that organized crime was untouchable.

"You may have a point," she said softly, watching the red sails of a small boat flutter in the wind.

"Of course I do. And by the way, I'm not going to be a mere captain much longer."

She dragged her eyes from the peaceful scene. "You're quitting?"

He frowned at her oddly hopeful expression. "Hardly. I'm going to be appointed chief of police."

As Kara felt her heart sink, she wondered what business it was of hers what the man wanted to do with his life. "When?"

"Next month, when the current chief retires. We're keeping the news under wraps until then."

"Is it what you really want?"

Adam looked at her with surprise. If he hadn't known better, he would have thought Kara shared Colin's disapproval of his latest career move. But that was impossible: she was a woman, after all. A delightful, enchanting one, granted, but when it came right down to it, weren't all females sisters under the skin, insisting that their men be constant achievers? Marilyn had certainly believed that she deserved better than an ordinary street cop.

If Adam were to be perfectly honest, he would have to admit that his former wife's wishes had provided the impetus for his climb up the departmental ladder. After his divorce, it had not escaped his notice that women were far more interested in a police lieutenant than in a mere patrolman. By the time he had made captain, his theory concerning the so-called gentler sex had been confirmed time and time again.

"Of course it is," he insisted. "I've worked hard for this, Kara. I deserve it. And I want it."

If he seemed to be protesting a bit too much, Kara decided not to remark on it. "I don't know what's come over me lately," she said with an apologetic smile. "It must be the full moon."

"The full moon was last week."

"Blame it on the waning moon, then. Or the tides. Did you know that seventy percent of the human body is water and that the very same percentage of water makes up the earth's surface? How can we not be affected by things like tides?"

Her eyes were too bright, her tone too brittle. Adam had made the false assumption that Kara Tiernan was one of those blissful souls who drift through life without a care in the world. He'd been way off the track. Something was very, very wrong.

"How indeed?" he responded easily, not thinking a public restaurant the best place to discuss what was obviously a personal topic.

Something was affecting both of them. And Adam knew damned well that the tension that arose between them without warning and with increasing frequency could not be attributed to moons or tides or any other such fanciful notion.

As if by mutual consent, they turned the conversation to lighter, less controversial topics—the weather, recent films, whether San Francisco or Kauai could boast the best sea-food restaurants.

They were lingering over coffee when a tall, stunning blonde, clad in a pair of amazingly brief shorts and a red-and-white striped halter top stopped at their table. "Kara," she said without preamble, "I'm so glad I found you."

"I've been trying to reach *you* since last night," Kara responded with a welcoming smile. "I want you to meet Adam Lassiter. Adam, this is Liz Forsythe, my very best friend."

"It's nice to meet you, Liz," Adam said, extending his hand. "And congratulations. Although it's 'best wishes' for the bride, isn't it?"

"Hi." The woman's eyes skimmed over Adam as she ignored his outstretched hand. "Kara, I have to talk to you. Now."

Kara's brow furrowed. Despite the fact that Liz was head over heels in love with Brett Britton, Kara had never seen her friend so upset that she'd so pointedly ignore any male, especially one as handsome as Adam.

"Sure," she said, pulling out a chair. "Why don't you join us for coffee?"

As Liz's distressed eyes returned to Adam, he got the message. Loud and clear. "I think I'll walk down to the beach," he said, tossing some bills onto the table. "Why don't you catch up with me later, Kara?"

Kara's gray eyes thanked him silently as she nodded her agreement. Liz appeared to have forgotten that he existed.

He'd seen that look before, Adam mused as he walked along the edge of the wet sand. More times than he cared to count. Liz Forsythe was undoubtedly a stunning woman—when she wasn't scared out of her wits.

"You've been a cop too long, Lassiter," Adam muttered. "It was probably just some foolish female thing. Like the wrong wedding dress being delivered, or what color flowers to order for her bouquet."

Even as Adam told himself that, he couldn't quite make himself believe it. And Kara's solemn expression, as she walked toward him twenty minutes later, only corroborated his gut instinct that there was a great deal more to her friend's problem than a simple ceremonial mix-up.

"Brett's gone," Kara informed him as they returned up the beach to the Jeep. The rain had stopped and the fresh air was softened with the scent of flowers.

"You mean he bailed out of the wedding." *See*, he told himself. *So much for your gut instincts, hotshot.*

She shook her head. "No, I mean he's disappeared. Brett and Liz both own their own businesses in Kapaa. Liz's is Kauai Kandy and Brett runs a scuba shop, Pacific Paradise Adventures, next door. When he didn't come back two days ago from a charter to Maui, Liz thought he must've picked up another job."

"Sounds reasonable." From what little Adam had seen of the islands thus far, clocks and schedules appeared to carry very little weight. Kara's eyes were filled with worry. He'd seen that look before, too. Usually right before things went to hell. "But he's still not back," he guessed, knowing the answer.

"No. Liz is afraid that he's in some kind of trouble. She spent all last night looking for him. That's why I couldn't reach her."

"It's probably more likely that the job took longer than he first thought," Adam said reassuringly. "Maybe the original clients decided to extend their vacation. There are a lot of things that could explain this, Kara."

"But Brett wouldn't have just taken off like that without a word; he'd have known Liz would be worried sick."

Adam was momentarily distracted by the sight of her long, tanned legs as she climbed into the driver's seat. When he couldn't help speculating how they'd feel wrapped around his body, he experienced an uncomfortable tightening in his loins. It had been a long time since any woman had affected him in that way, and he wasn't certain he liked it: it implied a definite lack of self-control.

"There's always another explanation."

"Such as Brett changing his mind about the wedding?"

He reached across the small space between the seats and took her hand. "It's been known to happen, Kara."

"I've known Brett Britton since he first came to the island nine months ago. He adores Liz. He wouldn't jilt her."

Once again her words sounded so very familiar. Adam wondered vaguely how many distressed women he'd seen come into the station, certain that something terrible had happened to their husband, lover, fiancé, significant other—whatever they were calling them these days. Ninety-nine percent of the time the guy had just gotten his fill of domestic life and split.

"Has she gone to the police?"

Kara made a sound of sheer disgust. "They agree with you."

When his only response was an arched brow, Kara elaborated. "That he's left her."

"It happens, Kara," Adam said quietly. "Even in paradise."

Jerking her hand from his, Kara twisted the key in the ignition. "Not here," she insisted firmly as she turned the Jeep back toward the highway. "And not with Liz and Brett."

A moment later she shot him a speculative, sideways glance. He could practically see the wheels turning inside that gorgeous red head.

"Adam, I have the most marvelous idea."

"No."

"You don't even know what I'm going to say," she complained.

"You're going to suggest that since the police refuse to look for Liz's missing fiancé, I volunteer my services."

She gave him a warm, persuasive smile. "I know you could do it, Adam. Don't forget I was there when you went into that warehouse and captured the armed robber. I thought you were the bravest, most amazing man I'd ever met."

"You sure as hell could've fooled me," he grumbled, remembering how he'd returned home that night flushed with success. Kara's sulky indifference had quickly burst his little bubble of self-congratulation.

"Surely you're not going to hold my foolish teenage behavior against me?"

"Of course I'm not. But that doesn't mean that I'm going to go off on any wild-goose chase for your friend's missing scuba diver, either."

"But you *are* a policeman."

"I'm also on vacation, as you keep pointing out."

Kara glanced over at him, undeterred by the grim line of his jaw. "Surely it wouldn't take that long—"

"Kara," he warned in a low, serious voice.

"All right," she said as she returned her attention to the winding road. "But I don't know what I'm going to tell poor Liz."

He stared at her. "Don't tell me you already volunteered my help."

The sophisticated demeanor Adam had adopted over the years suddenly slipped, giving Kara a glimpse of a blatantly uncivilized anger that gave her a very good idea of how the victims of the Spanish Inquisition must have felt.

"Oh, look," she said brightly. "Coming up on your right is Lumahei Beach; you'll probably recognize it because Hollywood shoots South Seas scenes there all the time. Most people consider it the prettiest beach in all of Hawaii. Of course other people argue that Hanalei Bay, where we had lunch, is prettiest. Did I tell you that's where they filmed *South Pacific*?"

"You did. But right now I'm more interested in what you told your friend."

"Honestly, Adam," Kara complained, "you really do need to learn to relax."

A moment later, Adam was treated to a scene lovely beyond praise. The velvet-green mountain and its golden coral sand, fringed by pandanus trees, was separated from the vast blue Pacific by a long ruffle of dazzling foam. The vista evoked all the mystical beauty of the South Seas. It also served to reduce his exasperation.

"Paradise found," he murmured.

Kara gave him a distinctly wary but appreciative glance. "Isn't it?"

She pulled off the road and cut the engine. Draping her wrists over the top of the steering wheel, she gazed out over the sun-brightened sea.

"Sometimes, when I'm feeling down, I'll come up here and just sit on the beach, watching the waves. Before long, I'll believe in the magic again."

Adam slipped his arm loosely over the back of her seat. "That's important to you, isn't it? The magic?"

He could hear her soft, rippling sigh. "This will probably only reconfirm your feeling that I'm as loosely wired

as Daffy Duck, but yes, I do believe in the magic. Sometimes it's the only way I know to get through the day."

Her solemnly spoken words cut through to some hidden
core within him. He had not expected such a serious answer to what had been an idle question. He studied her
profile carefully, unwillingly intrigued by this new aspect
of Colin's sister. As far as he had been able to tell, Kara lived
the carefree existence of a wood nymph; what could she
possibly know about hardship?

Yet it would have been impossible not to detect a lingering note of pain in her soft voice. Day by day, moment by
moment, he found himself growing more and more fasci-
nated.

"Are you still mad at me?" she asked softly. "I know I
acted outrageously, telling Liz that you'd help her find Brett,
but she was so upset, and Colin's always telling me that
you're the smartest policeman in all of California, so when
the idea popped into my head, I just blurted it out."

Her expression was so earnest that Adam couldn't resist
a smile. "I suppose I could talk to her," he agreed reluctantly.

She demurely lowered her eyes to keep him from seeing
her satisfaction. "That's very nice of you, Adam. Remind
me to reward you for this display of gallantry."

He lifted her chin. "I have every intention of doing exactly that." Their lips touched once. Briefly. Lightly. When
she tilted her head to press her lips against his at a new angle, Adam deepened the kiss degree by glorious degree. The
salt-tinged sea air filled her head, mingling erotically with
a rich, musky scent emanating from Adam's sun-warmed
skin as Kara wrapped her arms around him, delighting in
the way the pressure of his lips was continually changing—
first hard and heated, then soft and tantalizing.

When the tip of his tongue traced the curve of her upper lip, she moaned; when his teeth captured her lower lip, she trembled. When she ran her hands through his hair, the gesture fitted her body more closely to his, causing her breasts to yield to the strength of his chest.

"If this is the reward I get for agreeing to talk to your friend, I can't wait for the payoff when I find the guy," he said, touching his lips to her temple.

Kara closed her eyes briefly, luxuriating in the feel of his lips against her skin. "Then you do believe that something's happened to him? That he hasn't really jilted Liz?"

"I believe Liz believes that," Adam hedged.

"But you don't." Before he could respond, Kara shook her head firmly. "Please don't answer that until after you've talked with her and heard the story firsthand," she pleaded a little desperately.

"I suppose that's next on the agenda?" Personally, Adam could think of a great many better ways to spend a lazy afternoon with Kara.

"No, Liz has to go to Oahu tonight—something about a mix-up with the company that supplies her candy flavoring—so you're meeting her tomorrow morning for breakfast at the Kopper Kettle. For now, how do you feel about meeting a true *kamaaina*?"

Although Adam found it extremely odd that Liz Forsythe would be more worried about candy flavoring than her missing fiancé, he decided not to press the point. Perhaps Kara's friend was simply more pragmatic than she had appeared at first glance. Whatever, he was grateful for Liz's sudden trip to the neighboring island. It left him free to spend the evening with Kara.

"Depends on what a true *kamaaina* is. Animal, vegetable or mineral?"

"Precisely translated, it means 'child of the soil.' We use it to refer to someone who was born here. Or at the very least, who's lived here a long time. It's sort of like being in *Burke's Peerage*," she explained, as if it were important that Adam understand the honor she was bestowing on him.

He glanced down at his rain-rumpled clothing. "I'm not sure I'm properly dressed to meet royalty."

As Kara's gray eyes swept over him, she surprised him by agreeing. "You're right.... No problem," she announced, starting the Jeep. "We can stop on the way."

Thirty minutes later, a lush lavender vanda orchid lei around his neck, Adam followed Kara through a winding maze of overgrown rosebushes toward a house that was an oddly eclectic mishmash of architectural styles.

Constructed of red brick, it might have been New England in feeling, had there not been huge white marble columns out front, and a wide porch, which gave it an antebellum air. A series of Victorian cupolas rose from a Spanish tile roof. It was as if the unfortunate house had changed hands several times in the construction process, each new owner adding his own imprint, rather than scrapping previous plans and starting afresh.

They were led into a screened solarium, filled to abundance with tropical plants. The atmosphere in the room was torrid—moist enough, Adam was certain, to grow mushrooms through the bleached plank flooring. His head swam with the sweet scent of the vivid hothouse flowers.

Adam's attention was immediately drawn past a towering banana plant to an ancient woman, seated regally in a bamboo peacock throne chair. Despite the sweltering heat, her spare frame was bundled in a shawl of soft Scottish wool. Antique gold rings adorned every finger, and the woman's wispy hair was an extraordinary shade of lavender, blending with her bright pink scalp into a pastel tapestry. A head lei made of a variety of ferns and brilliant scarlet and citron flowers circled her head.

The entire scene—the jungle plants, the ancient woman, the uniformed Oriental houseboy standing protectively beside her—all evoked some long-past era.

However, the vast assortment of electronic equipment—state-of-the-art video cameras, wide-screen television, videocassette recorders, high-powered telescopes—might have come from the prop department of the most recent James Bond adventure.

"I don't think I'm in Kansas any longer," Adam murmured.

"Speak up, young man." The woman's voice was high but strong.

"I was just commenting on your equipment."

"Isn't it nice? Ling Su brings me the latest catalogs, and I order whatever is new on the market."

The woman's eyes turned to Kara. "It's about time you brought a man home," she said, holding out her arms.

Kara knelt beside the chair, giving the ancient woman a hug as she pressed a light kiss against her weathered cheek.

"It's not what you think, Grandy," she protested softly. "I'm just showing Adam the island and thought you'd enjoy meeting one of Colin's friends."

She stood up again, gesturing toward Adam. "Grandy, this is Adam Lassiter. Adam, this is my grandmother."

The old woman's eyes filled with avid interest. "So you're one of Colin's friends, are you? Do you know that rascal of a grandson hasn't visited me in nearly a year?"

Since he hadn't known Colin even had a grandmother, it would have been a bit difficult for Adam to have been aware of that fact. "I'm sorry," he said.

She shot him a severe glance. "Whatever for? I'm sure it isn't your fault my family chooses to ignore me."

"Colin calls you every Sunday, Grandy," Kara pointed out.

The old woman gave an unfeminine snort. "Telephones. Blasted newfangled equipment isn't the same as a real flesh-and-blood visit."

"Spoken by the woman who's keeping the Japanese economy afloat single-handedly," Kara countered dryly, glancing around the electronics-filled room. "Is that new?" she asked, indicating a black-and-chrome entertainment center that looked as though it could have come from the bridge of the Starship Enterprise.

"Just arrived yesterday," the elderly woman confirmed with a broad smile. "This little baby just happens to be cable equipped for 134 channels. Stereo, of course," she said, directing her words to Adam.

"Of course," he agreed without missing a beat.

"It's also got Dolby noise reduction, high-speed dubbing and a fourteen-band equalizer." She cackled delightedly as she rubbed her beringed hands together. "Old Sturm und Drang only has a five-band equalizer. He'll die from envy when he sees this." Her sparkling eyes laughed up at the houseboy, who thus far had remained silent. "Won't he, Ling Su?"

"He'll keel over with first sight, Missy Maggie," the young Oriental man answered serenely, nodding his dark head.

"Sturm und Drang is Grandy's nickname for Maximilian Heinrich von Schiller," Kara explained under her breath in answer to Adam's questioning glance. "He was one of her early directors. In fact, Max takes credit for launching Grandy to stardom."

Despite her advanced years, Kara's grandmother proved her hearing was still that of a young girl by overhearing Kara's murmured explanation.

"Horsefeathers!" she spat out, banging an intricately carved ivory-topped cane imperiously on the floor. "If anything, it was I who saved Max from drowning in that overly dramatic stew he was making of *Pride and Prejudice*."

"You're Maggie Tiernan," Adam said, suddenly recognizing Kara's grandmother.

Maggie Tiernan, he recalled from a college film class he'd taken his junior year at San Francisco University, had exuded an incredible amount of sex appeal, suggesting more with her eyes than anything today's scriptwriters could pen for an actress. Her star had taken off like a blazing comet when her studio dubbed her their Sizzle Girl, and by 1914, Maggie was reportedly making a mind-boggling salary of $2,000 a week.

Then, on October 6, 1927, her star had crashed to earth. In a Broadway theater, far from the Hollywood set where Maggie was acting out the role of Elizabeth, the Virgin Queen, viewers were watching Al Jolson in *The Jazz Singer*. The immediate success of that first talking feature film had marked the end of an era. Maggie's high, wispy voice had not been able to survive the temperamental performance of early microphones. She'd retired, becoming more reclusive as she grew older.

"That's me. I'll bet you thought I'd died years ago," Maggie Tiernan added with the forthrightness usually attributed to either the very young or the very elderly.

"Of course not," Adam responded on cue, not quite truthfully, as he sat down in a wicker chair the houseboy had retrieved from a corner of the solarium.

"Of course you did. And now you're face-to-face with this very silly old woman who observes the world through a television screen, and you're wondering why you're here."

"I thought Adam would enjoy meeting a native," Kara cut in before Adam could respond.

Adam thought it was interesting that Kara did not mention her belief that he'd been sent here to seduce her. She certainly hadn't had any qualms about telling her parents, he mused, wondering at her change in tactics.

Maggie gave her granddaughter a very knowing look, pausing just long enough for dramatic effect. *She's still quite an actress*, Adam reflected with appreciation for the outlandish scene Maggie had cast them all in. Of course, after meeting the other members of the Tiernan family, Adam was not as surprised as he might have been by Kara's grandmother's eccentricities.

"You've always been a terrible liar, young lady," Maggie retorted. "Besides, I didn't just fall off the pineapple truck, you know."

She waved her hand dismissively as Kara opened her mouth to protest. "However, since you and Adam are not prepared to make an announcement quite yet, we'll overlook the matter. For now."

"Grandmother, you are incorrigible." Kara's tone was firm, but a smile teased at the corners of her mouth.

"I certainly hope so, my dear," Maggie agreed. "It's just about the only fun left to an old lady. Speaking of aging, my mind must be going soft: I haven't offered your young man refreshments. Ling Su, please prepare some of your excellent Oriental brew," she commanded with the regal demeanor of a deposed Russian empress.

"Of course, Missy Maggie. Right away." The young man obediently left the room.

"Now. Down to business." The elderly woman peered at Adam with bright black eyes that reminded him of a curious bird's. "I've heard Kara's feeble explanation; why don't you tell me the real reason you're here."

"Colin sent me down here to seduce Kara for her birthday," he answered immediately, ignoring Kara's blazing look.

The still-bright button eyes swept over Kara, subjecting her granddaughter to a long, studied appraisal. "Colin always did have exquisite taste in gifts," Maggie acknowledged, repeating Michael Tiernan's words of the previous evening. "I may just forgive him for not visiting me."

"Adam is only kidding, Grandy," Kara insisted. "Tell her that you're only joking," she demanded, glaring at Adam.

Adam was fast discovering that he enjoyed seeing Kara flustered. The soft pink color infusing her cheeks was decidedly attractive, and her gray eyes, alive with furious passion, were a gleaming silver.

"But I'm not certain I am," he objected, stretching his legs out in front of him as he folded his arms over his stomach and subjected Kara to a slow, leisurely inspection. "Actually, the more I think about it, the more I find the idea vastly appealing."

Kara stared at the sudden devilry dancing in Adam's blue eyes. For the second time in the past hour she was forced to wonder where she had ever gotten the idea that this man was harmless. Despite his formal clothing and disciplined behavior, she suddenly had the feeling that he could be every bit as unmanageable as her grandmother and her parents admittedly were. Or her brother. For the first time since his arrival on Kauai, Kara could actually envision Colin and this man as friends.

Adam watched, satisfied as slow recognition dawned in her eyes. He hadn't enjoyed being treated like some tame pet to be kept obediently at heel. He decided it was high time that he began to set the rules. That Kara had acknowledged his decision was enough. For now.

Maggie's interested gaze had not missed the exchange between Kara and Adam. "I like this one," she announced, sounding once again like her son. "He knows how to add zest to the chase."

Her ebony eyes sparkled up at Adam. "There was a time when I would have enjoyed fighting that age-old battle of the sexes with you, Adam Lassiter."

He leaned forward, taking her creased hand and raising it to his smiling lips. "Believe me, Miss Tiernan, if you'd honored me with your interest, we wouldn't have wasted our time fighting."

Kara's mouth dropped open, and all she could do was stare as Maggie giggled like a schoolgirl. Kara didn't know whose behavior astounded her more—Adam's or her grandmother's. Whichever, Kara had no more time to dwell on it as Ling Su returned with a tea tray, distracting Maggie's attention once again.

"Thank you, Ling Su. Everything looks lovely, as usual." She turned toward Kara and Adam as the young man poured the steaming, fragrant brew.

"Nobody knows how to brew tea like the Orientals. It's the pot, you know. They heat it first with boiling water. Then they stir the leaves ever so gently, taking care not to bruise them. Tea leaves are very delicate. Only a master brewer knows precisely how much pressure to apply in order to waken the full flavor without damaging the surface. Bruised leaves give tea a bitter taste. Isn't that correct, Ling Su?" she asked brightly.

"That's right, Missy Maggie." The young man bowed with all the polite servitude of his ancestors.

Adam watched as the woman sipped the tea with the air of a wine connoisseur sampling a vintage cabernet sauvignon. "Excellent, as usual," she proclaimed finally.

"You appear to know a great deal about tea," Adam said, nodding his thanks to Ling Su as the servant handed him a delicate china cup decorated with hand-painted violets.

"I should. After all, I did play the great Kublai Khan's wife in *The Adventures of Marco Polo*."

"I saw that just last week," Adam surprised both women by saying.

Kara slanted him a look that, though one of gratitude, told him he needn't bother to lie. Adam steadfastly ignored her.

"You were the best thing in the movie," he continued. "I especially liked that part where you got down on your knees and begged your husband not to kill Marco Polo. Were those real tears?"

Maggie bobbed her pastel head. "Of course. I never resorted to using fake tears. I was an actress. Not like these young girls these days. All they seem to know how to do is take off their clothes and spout obscenities."

She snorted. "To think they invented talking pictures just so people could sit in a theater and listen to cursing. It makes you wonder if that's what the industry had in mind."

Kara had heard all this before, and as interesting as she had always found her grandmother's colorful tales, she allowed her thoughts to drift as Maggie gave Adam a lengthy discourse on the days of silent pictures.

Kara was honestly surprised by how instantly Adam had taken to her eccentric grandmother. She had expected him to be polite, of course—she never would have submitted her beloved Grandy to deliberate rudeness. Reluctantly Kara admitted that introducing Adam first to her parents, and today to her grandmother, were acts of self-protection.

She had wanted to establish boundaries, to prove to him that no matter how strong the physical attraction between them, there was absolutely nothing on which they could ever expect to base a relationship.

Oil and water. That's what they were. Shake swiftly and they might come together for a short time, but that's all it could be. What on earth could Colin have been thinking of, she wondered. And from her grandmother's reaction to Adam, Kara knew that Maggie Tiernan shared her grandson's unfortunate inclination toward matchmaking.

Deciding that it was time to return home before her grandmother had her and Adam engaged, Kara replaced her teacup on the gold-rimmed saucer with more force than necessary. Both Adam and Maggie turned toward her.

"We should be getting back," she said in answer to Adam's questioning look.

It was impossible to miss her frosty tone, and Adam wondered at its cause. He rose immediately.

"Thank you, Miss Tiernan," he said, taking her hand. "It's been a pleasure."

"Will you come back?" Her eyes betrayed a hint of pleading.

"I'll be back," Adam promised, brushing his lips against the back of her veined hand. He slipped the orchid lei off and slipped it over the elderly woman's head. "If you promise more tea."

She nodded happily as she fingered the lavender flowers. "I knew you'd like the tea. Ling Su does such an excellent job of preparation."

"You've a real fan in there, Ling Su," Adam said to the young man as he accompanied them back through the rosebush maze to the Jeep.

"Call me Larry. I only use Ling Su when I'm doing my Oriental houseboy routine."

Adam stared down at the young man who'd dropped all trace of accented speech. "You're as American as I am."

"Sure," he said blithely. "I was born in L.A. In fact, my family has lived in the San Fernando Valley for over a hundred years, except for the time in an internment camp up north during the war. I went to Hollywood High, then UCLA and got my master's in international banking at USC."

Adam eyed the young man with renewed interest. "And you're working as a houseboy to a doddering old silent film star? No offense, Kara," Adam said quickly as he caught Kara's angry intake of breath at his ungallant description of her grandmother.

Larry "Ling Su" Lee shrugged. "Hey, don't knock it. The old lady pays a helluva salary. She's been through fifteen different servants in the past three years. I'm the first one willing to put up with her flaky stories and treat her like a star."

"That's true," Kara admitted. "Grandy's a doll—I truly love her—but she goes back and forth between the past and future sometimes without warning." She smiled up at Maggie's house servant. "Larry has amazing patience."

"What do you get out of it?" Adam asked.

"Room and board and a salary that rivals a Bank of America vice president's. I've been doing some pretty heavy investing and figure I'll be able to retire before I'm thirty. I also get plenty of time off for surfing.

"Plus," he admitted with a slight show of embarrassment, "I kinda like her. Maggie's a little weird, but she's nice. And things are definitely more interesting since she's set up that communications center. Don't tell her I told you, but she's got half the valley bugged."

Adam shook his head in silent admiration. "Amazing. And the man can brew tea, as well."

Larry laughed. "If you dare tell, I'll deny it to my dying day," he warned, "but that stuff is nothing but Lipton tea bags. All it takes is a little imagination."

"And Grandy," Kara supplied, "has plenty of that to spare."

She was quiet as they drove back down the highway, returning the way they had come. To Adam's surprise, she drove at less than the speed of light and seemed thoughtful. Deciding that she needed time to digest the subtle change in their relationship, he also remained silent, content to watch the scenery.

It was incredible, he mused, now able to understand Kara's apparent belief in magic. Jagged mountains sloped down to gorgeous bays through valleys carpeted with sugarcane and pineapple and dappled by shafts of reflected sunlight. The narrow winding road curved through lazy, sun-drenched villages where placid Buddhas kept eternal watch in Oriental cemeteries. Wind and wave, rain and river had sculpted the tropical island into a kind of fairy-like reality that was magical. Adam almost found himself believing in the mystic powers of rainbows.

"Thank you," she said after a time.

The sun was painting the sky saffron, and Adam had to drag his attention away from the brilliant sunset. "For what?"

"For being nice to my grandmother."

He shrugged off her appreciation. "She was easy to be nice to; I liked her. Actually, now that you bring it up, Kara, I like your entire family. A lot."

That wasn't supposed to be how her test turned out. He was supposed to be shocked by her family's individual and collective eccentricities. Appalled. He wasn't supposed to want anything further to do with her. This new Adam Lassiter, the future San Francisco chief of police, was supposed to prove himself to be nothing more than a stiff, pompous ass. Damn. It was against the rules for him to be nice.

"You didn't have to lie about seeing Marco Polo."

"I didn't."

She narrowed her eyes. "Give me a break here, Adam. You may be able to fool an old lady, but not me."

"I saw the film at a silent film festival the Police Benevolent Association sponsored for charity," he answered amiably. "Your grandmother's efforts contributed to a lot of beds for San Francisco's homeless."

"Oh."

"Oh," he mimicked. He reached out, putting his hand lightly, unthreateningly on her thigh. "What are the plans for the evening?"

"Evening?"

"Evening. You know, that quiet, romantic time after the sun goes down. When the world slows down to catch its breath. Evening," he repeated patiently.

She glanced over at him in surprise. "Since the twilight dinner sail is obviously out, I hadn't made any other plans."

Truthfully, after meeting her grandmother, she had thought he wouldn't have been able to get away from her soon enough. Obviously, Kara realized, she had miscalculated.

Adam ruffled her hair in a carefree, affectionate gesture. "Don't worry," he said with a bold grin. "I'm sure I can think of something."

Kara found the unexpected turn of events, not to mention his provocatively husky tone and the lambent flame gleaming in Adam's deep blue eyes, far from comforting.

Strangely light-headed, she returned her attention to her driving, ignoring Adam's deep, self-satisfied chuckle.

7

ADAM FELT HIS PLANS for a romantic evening for two disintegrate like fog under a bright Hawaiian sun when they approached the cottage and found Michael Tiernan waiting on the front lanai.

"Aha!" Michael called out, waving his hat in welcome. "You're back. I was just getting ready to leave."

Adam cursed his decision not to have Kara stop so he could take a picture of the neatly squared rice paddies and taro patches along the Hanalei River. From the vantage point afforded by the highway, the peaceful scene had reminded him remarkably of the Orient. If they'd only stopped for five minutes—three, even—he could have avoided what he knew was going to be a long evening listening to Kara's father wax philosophical about the arts.

"I brought the painting," Michael said, lifting up a large, bulky package wrapped in brown paper and tied with string. His next words confirmed Adam's worst fears. "As well as a portfolio of some of my favorite sketches. I thought as a fellow art aficionado, you'd undoubtedly enjoy an artist's view of the island."

Adam ignored Kara's low chuckle. "I can't think of anything I'd enjoy more," he said weakly.

Kara patted his arm. "Have fun," she said cheerily as she turned to head down the beach to her own cottage.

Unwilling to allow her to escape quite yet, Adam wrapped his fingers around her wrist. "What would you say to my dropping by for a nightcap after your father leaves?"

His words seemed to be a request, but a silent demand swirled in the depths of his eyes. Once again Kara was forced to remind herself that Adam Lassiter deserved his reputation as a tough no-nonsense police officer. That silent, unblinking stare was admittedly intimidating. She knew that were she being interrogated by Captain Lassiter, she'd have a difficult time resisting it.

"Sorry," she said with far more aplomb than she was feeling, "I'm going to bed early; I have to work tomorrow."

Adam could feel the satisfaction flowing through him, comforting and stimulating at the same time. "Putting in my tile." He found the idea of Kara puttering around the cottage all day extremely pleasing.

"No, not that."

His fingers tightened. "What do you mean, no?"

The sudden storm rising in his eyes belied his low tone. Kara pried away the strong fingers circling her wrist. She refused to allow him to frighten her with that silent air of intimidation.

"*No*," she repeated firmly. "A two-letter word used to express negation, dissent, denial or refusal. Are you going to let go of me?"

"No." He gave her a grim smile as his fingers tightened around her wrist. "You see, I do know what the word means, Kara. What I'd like is an explanation of why you're not coming over here tomorrow to finish your work."

Kara knew Adam didn't give a damn about the tile. He was interested in her. "I only do that sort of work in my spare time," she said, tossing her head furiously. "And then it's just as a favor for my family. And friends." Her haughty tone dismissed him from the latter group.

"If you're not the island handyman, what do you do for a real job?"

Well, Kara decided, here was the ultimate test. She took a deep breath. "I write questions for television game shows."

Adam told himself not to stare. He failed. Miserably. "You do what?"

"I write questions for quiz shows. Do you have a problem with that?" Kara waited for him to offer some disparaging remark, but not for the first time, Adam surprised her.

"Actually," he said slowly, rubbing his chin as he looked down at her, "I can't think of a better job for someone who still hasn't made her mind up what she wants to do when she grows up."

In spite of her irritation at his overbearing attitude, Kara couldn't stop her lips from betraying the faintest hint of a smile. "You've been talking to Colin again."

"Guilty. Just a short nightcap, Kara. That's all I'm suggesting."

His words might be saying one thing, but the message in his eyes was something else altogether. "I'm really exhausted, Adam," she protested quietly. "Besides, you have to get up early to have breakfast with Liz, remember?"

"What time?" he asked resignedly, knowing that the entire meeting was going to be nothing but a waste of time. He'd listen to Kara's friend's story, dry her tears, if it came to that, then, after assuring her that she was too good a woman for this Britton character, he'd be on his way. To Kara.

"Ten. Call me after you talk to her?"

Ten was early? Not wanting to get into another argument over their obvious differences in life-styles, Adam merely nodded. "Of course."

She smiled up at him. "Thank you, Adam. This is really very nice of you."

He shrugged. "Thank you for the tour."

"Don't mention it. Far be it from me to give you the idea that we islanders aren't overflowing with the aloha spirit."

For not the first time since meeting Kara, Adam felt unreasonably powerless as she turned on her heel and began jogging down the expanse of coral sand.

"She's more complex than she appears at first glance," Michael offered as he came up beside Adam. "People look at Kara and fall in love with the free spirit, never guessing there's an intelligent, flesh-and-blood woman living inside that attractive packaging."

Adam didn't feel it prudent to tell Michael Tiernan that what he was feeling for the man's daughter was a great deal more basic than love.

"She's got a lot of her grandmother in her," he murmured thoughtfully instead.

Michael looked at him with renewed interest. "So she took you to meet Maggie, did she? What did you think?"

Adam paused, choosing his words carefully. "I think that you must have had an extremely interesting childhood."

Michael threw back his head and laughed heartily. "What a wonderfully circumspect answer," he said, throwing a friendly arm around Adam's shoulders. "*Interesting*," he chortled. "That's one word for it."

They entered the cottage and were sipping drinks—Adam his usual Scotch, Michael white rum on ice—when Kara's father suddenly turned the conversation away from the island sights Kara had shown Adam.

"I'm a bastard, you know."

Adam wasn't fooled for a moment by Michael's casual tone. The gleam in those intelligent blue eyes showed he was waiting for an answer. It was a test, and both men knew it.

"You shouldn't be so hard on yourself," Adam drawled, eyeing the expectant man over the rim of his glass. "From what I've witnessed so far, you're an amiable enough man."

Michael nodded, accepting the ball as it returned to his court. "That's what all my patients say," he acknowledged. "However, I was speaking in the biblical sense. My mother was never married to my father."

Adam shrugged, unconcerned. "So?"

It could have been his imagination, but Adam thought he detected the slightest expression of relief flicker in the depths of those strangely observant blue eyes. "It ruffled a few feathers back in those days. Probably still would disturb some individuals. It doesn't bother you?"

"No," Adam answered honestly. "Does it bother you?"

"Of course not," Michael answered impatiently. "But as you've already pointed out, my childhood was not exactly the norm. Maggie's circle of friends could be described as bohemian at best. And more than one of my surrogate relatives was blacklisted during the McCarthy era."

Adam thought he knew where this was going. He put the glass down on a rattan chair beside the table. Leaning back, he rested his elbows on the bamboo arm of the chair and linked his fingers together.

"We're not really discussing your parentage here, are we?"

Appearing suddenly uncomfortable, Michael Tiernan threw back his head, tossing back the rum in rapid gulps. When he returned his gaze to Adam, he was no longer smiling.

Adam had seen that same expression on Kara's face from time to time. Secrets, he mused. The Tiernan family definitely had its share.

"She's my daughter, Adam. And I love her."

"I'm sure you do. A woman like Kara would be easy to love."

Michael stared down at his empty glass, as if wishing it could magically be refilled. Then he lifted his head to give Adam a warning look.

"I don't want her hurt," he said quietly, with a forcefulness that was at direct odds with the cheery, carefree character Adam had been introduced to the night before.

"What makes you think I'd do anything to hurt her?"

"You probably wouldn't mean to," Michael allowed. "But you're going to. I can see it coming, and damned if I know how to stop it."

"I didn't realize all the Tiernans possessed second sight," Adam said dryly, annoyed at Michael's rather presumptuous pronouncement.

"I'm not as young as I once was, but I've got a damned good memory," Michael countered. "And my eyesight is every bit as good as it used to be; I don't need second sight to see the romance blooming between you and Kara, and as her father, I have a responsibility to try to head off trouble before it gets out of hand. There's no future for you and my daughter; what police chief would want a wife whose paternal grandmother testified before the House Un-American Activities Committee?"

Irritated by the obvious fact that he'd been the subject of conversation between Colin and Michael Tiernan, Adam arched a blond brow.

"Are you asking me my intentions?"

"I'm asking you not to use my daughter as a vacation diversion," Michael responded with a sudden burst of heat. "Something to pass the time before you return to San Francisco and pick up the reins of your career."

"I'm not going to force Kara into anything she doesn't want," Adam said tightly. "She's a grown woman, capable of making her own decisions. I don't want to argue with you, Michael, but our relationship really isn't any of your concern."

Michael dragged his hand wearily over his face. "I didn't think it would work," he muttered as he rose and made his way to the door.

"Then why did you bother to make the attempt?"

He turned in the doorway, looking as if he had suddenly aged a lifetime. "She's my child," he said simply. "I love her."

With that he was gone, taking his portfolio, but leaving the wrapped painting. Adam stood in the doorway, watching until Kara's father was out of sight. Then, picking up the telephone, he began dialing.

COLIN TIERNAN pushed his hand through his thick black hair as the telephone across the room rang for what had to be the hundredth time that day. He'd been working on the same chapter for the past two days; the last thing he needed was another interruption. Leaving the untimely caller to his answering machine, Colin continued to stare doggedly out over the windswept cliffs of Big Sur, demanding his muse to come through and help him out of the corner he had managed to write himself into.

"What the hell is going on?"

As the gritty sound of his best friend's voice shattered his concentration, Colin swore softly and picked up the receiver.

"Hello to you, too," he answered. "I hope you realize that you're interrupting a literary genius at work."

"That's nothing compared to what you've done to me," Adam complained. "I thought you sent me down here to relax."

"That was the idea," Colin agreed easily as he began doodling idly on a legal pad beside the phone.

"So how can I relax when I'm surrounded by your crazy family?"

"They're getting to you, huh?" Colin asked with a low chuckle. "Which ones?"

"Which ones?" Adam repeated. "Name one who isn't. I take that back," he said after a fleeting moment's consideration. "Your mother, so far, has been nothing but agreeable. However, it wouldn't surprise me in the least if she dropped in at any minute with some lightly veiled warning to keep my California cop's hands off your sister."

"She'd call first. Despite her rather artistic absentmindedness, my mother could give Miss Manners a lesson when it comes to social protocol." He paused to fill in some features on the woman's face he was absently sketching.

"So, speaking of my sister, how is Kara?" he asked, eyeing his work judiciously.

Although his writing paid for his rambling cliff-side home, Colin enjoyed sketching. His father had always claimed credit for that particular talent, and Colin had never thought it necessary to correct him.

"Frustrating as hell. Not that it matters," Adam growled, "since your father has already warned me away from her in no uncertain terms."

Colin widened the curve of the woman's upper lip, nodding his satisfaction as she appeared to be smiling back at him. "I thought it was strange when he called me a while ago," he murmured. "Pop usually stays out of our personal lives."

"I figured he'd spoken with you since last night. By the way, thanks for telling him about my promotion."

Colin ignored Adam's sarcasm. "I thought it might help improve your image. So what did you do to get my usually easygoing father so uptight?"

"Nothing yet." Adam's voice was sharp with obvious frustration.

"Aha." Colin added an arch to her brows before using the side of the pencil to draw in long dark waves that kissed her prominent cheekbones. "The plot thickens. I assume that Kara returns these feelings?"

Adam had already had enough lectures from the Tiernan men. He wasn't in the mood for another. "Are you asking as a friend? Or a brother?"

"That's a rough one. A friend," he decided. "I've already given you my big-brother spiel."

"I think she does. Correction, I *know* she does. But every time I begin to get close to her, she backs away."

"Give her time," Colin advised. "After all, Adam, you've only been on the island two days. Things move a little slower down there."

Adam had heard that little homily far too often lately. Since arriving on Kauai, he was discovering an impatient streak he had not been aware he possessed.

"So I've been told," he snapped.

"Then what's the problem?"

"To tell you the truth, I don't know exactly why I called."

Impulse, Adam mused. He'd done the first thing that came to mind. But that was ridiculous. He hadn't acted on impulse in years; Adam Lassiter was known for his ability to weigh every action carefully.

When was the last time he'd been driven to discuss his personal life with anyone, even his best friend? He and Colin regularly discussed careers, politics, the state of the world, and the Oakland, now Los Angeles, Raiders. But they had never, in his memory, had a conversation concerning either of their dealings with a woman. Not a specific one, at any rate.

Like most men, they only talked in generalities when it came to the opposite sex. What in the hell was Kara doing to his mind?

"I'm sorry about losing my temper," Adam said, suddenly feeling like a foolish, love-struck adolescent. "Thanks for listening."

"Hey, no problem," Colin answered absently.

"Get back to work." Adam recognized that tone. He'd just lost Kara's brother to whatever muse was whispering in his ear. "I'm sorry to have disturbed you."

Colin's only response was a vague murmured agreement. His attention was riveted on the striking woman who was staring up at him from the legal pad. It was undoubtedly only his imagination, but her wide dark eyes appeared to be shimmering with tears. He ripped off the page, crumpling it into a ball before tossing it in the direction of the wastepaper basket across the room.

Muttering an oath, he returned his attention to the computer screen, and was rewarded by the imagined sound of dogs baying eerily through a swirl of thick, icy Puget Sound fog. He was back on track. Immensely gratified, Colin began tapping away at the keys, the crumpled yellow lined paper on the oak floor entirely forgotten.

On the faraway island of Kauai, as the deserted beach outside his wide picture window caught the last moment of evening sun, Adam Lassiter pulled a thick manila file from his briefcase and went to work, determined to put Kara Tiernan and her colorful but highly distracting family out of his mind.

He spent most of the night and the early part of the morning poring over the thick sheaf of documents compiled by the commission staff. If Kara's face appeared before him more often than he would have liked, if he found himself gazing out the wide expanse of glass hoping for a glimpse of her, he refused to acknowledge that his interest was anything but casual. But as he left the house to meet Liz

Forsythe, Adam could not remember a single thing he'd read.

ADAM'S BREAKFAST MEETING with Liz Forsythe was brief and uninformative. He could see why the Kauai police chief had not been interested in her story. Despite the fact that Liz was an attractive intelligent woman, all the signs pointed to the conclusion that Britton had merely decided to try his luck somewhere else. After all, he'd spent eight years drifting around the South Pacific; the nine months he had spent on Kauai represented the longest time he'd settled anywhere. Obviously, with marriage right around the corner, he'd felt the noose of responsibility tightening around his neck and taken off before he suddenly found himself making mortgage payments. Or paying his income tax.

On the surface, that's all the case amounted to: another woman becoming a little wiser the hard way. But something had been nagging at the back of Adam's mind since Liz had first arrived at the café thirty minutes late, with some vague, obviously concocted reason for having been on Oahu. After insisting that Brett would not have jilted her, the young woman answered his questions unhesitatingly, gave him a recent photograph of Brett and promised to let him know if she remembered anything he might have said that would shed some light on his disappearance. She was nothing if not cooperative. And she was lying, Adam added as he drove the rental car up to Princeville.

Over the years he had heard a great many people lie, and for some inexplicable reason, he'd bet a month's salary that the lissome Liz Forsythe had been yet another who wasn't telling the truth. That she was hiding something was obvious. But what? And why? Adam found himself unwillingly intrigued.

He found Kara seated in a green meadow, surrounded by a group of wide-eyed children. Her cotton skirt, emblazoned with brilliant orange and gold poppies, billowed about her, making the flowers appear to have sprung from the fragrant volcanic earth. A creamy hibiscus was tucked behind her ear, a lei of cerise plumeria around her neck. Adam couldn't remember ever seeing anything quite so lovely.

"'He was a very nasty giant,'" she read aloud to the avid listeners, "'forever sticking his tongue out at people and calling them names.'"

"That's just like Tony," a young girl piped up.

"It's not either," an obviously rankled boy, whom Adam took to be the accused, argued.

"Is too."

"Not!"

"Is too," the girl repeated insistently.

"Hey," Kara broke in, "I thought you wanted to hear the story." Her tone, though soft, carried the unmistakable ring of authority. The two children fell silent.

Kara nodded. "That's better," she said with a smile.

"There! He did it again," Debbie Kaualua called out, pointing a finger at Tony as he stuck his tongue out at her.

"Tony," Kara admonished sternly, "that's enough. If you and Debbie don't stop squabbling, you'll both have to go home without hearing the end of the story. Is that understood?"

Eyes downcast, two dark heads nodded obediently.

"Now, where are we?" Kara murmured.

"The giant was calling people bad names," a helpful listener offered.

Kara flashed the boy an appreciative grin as she ruffled his dark hair. "Thank you, Paulo."

Adam noted with some amusement that the dazzling smile was no less effective on six-year-old boys than it was on grown men. A soft flush deepened the already dark tone of Paulo's skin as he appeared momentarily dumbfounded.

"Anyway," Kara continued, oblivious to Paulo's stunned reaction. "'People were getting very tired of this nasty, ill-tempered old giant. Finally another giant tossed the obnoxious fellow into the ocean where sharks ate every bit of him. Except his tongue. It was too bitter even for a shark to eat. They spit it back out and—'"

"It turned into the black rock on Lumahai Beach," someone broke in eagerly.

Kara rewarded her audience with a smile. "That's right."

"Read us another." The cry was taken up by the crowd of children, their young voices high and enthusiastic.

"Well, I suppose we have time for one more. Who wants to hear the legend of Spouting Horn?"

A flurry of hands shot up. All except one. "Who's that?" a little girl with sleek black hair and almond eyes inquired, pointing toward Adam.

As she lifted her head, Kara's gaze met Adam's steadily watchful one. A blush crept into her cheeks. "I think," she said slowly, "that we've read enough for today." The resultant complaints sounded like a Greek chorus of doomsayers, but one that Kara ignored.

"Nolina," she instructed the girl who had first taken note of Adam, "would you please tell Mrs. Yukimura that I'm going to take a short break and will be back in a little while?"

"Are you Kara's boyfriend?" the little girl asked, lingering behind to study Adam with somber, unblinking eyes.

Adam smiled down at her. "I'm working on it."

"Mr. Lassiter is a friend of my brother's," Kara snapped with uncharacteristic irritation. "Now scoot. If you're a good girl, maybe Mrs. Yukimura will let you date-stamp the books."

Apparently she had said the magic words; the young girl took off like a shot, leaving Kara and Adam alone. For a moment, neither seemed particularly inclined toward casual conversation.

"If you've come for a library card, Rose could have helped you," Kara said finally.

"I'm sure she could have," Adam agreed. "Mrs. Yukimura seemed quite accommodating; she was the one who told me where to find you."

He hadn't moved toward her; a gap of at least three feet separated them. So why could she feel the warmth of his gaze heating her body?

"I thought you were supposed to be researching questions."

"Lupe Kee, the children's librarian, is in bed with a touch of the flu," Kara explained. "I volunteered to help out with the weekly story hour."

"You're quite an accommodating lady."

She began gathering up the books scattered on the grass. "Why are you here, Adam? If it's about Liz and Brett, you could have simply called me this evening. And if your roof leaked during last night's rain, all I can do for today is lend you a bucket."

"I missed you."

Those three simple words stopped her in midsentence. Giving up on collecting the books of Hawaiian folklore, Kara stood up. She stuck her hands into the pockets of her flowered skirt as she turned away, her eyes riveted on the aquamarine water beyond the edge of the towering cliff.

"Tell me about your meeting with Liz," she said after a moment.

Adam would not have thought that there were very many things capable of unnerving Kara. He decided he liked the idea of being one of them.

"How long have you known Elizabeth Forsythe?"

"We've been best friends since fourth grade. Why?"

"Do you know of any reason she'd lie about her boyfriend's vanishing act?"

"Lie?" She shook her head. "Liz doesn't lie."

"She did this morning."

"I don't understand!" she exclaimed, turning to face him. "Are you saying that Liz knows where Brett's gone?"

The warm Hawaiian sun was reflected in her hair, and unable to resist, Adam ran his hand down the molten copper strands. "I didn't say that. But she knows a helluva lot more than she's telling.... I thought of you, Kara. All night. Last night and the one before that; I couldn't get you out of my mind."

Her mouth went suddenly dry. She swallowed. "You certainly don't sound very happy about it."

He swore softly, then pulled Kara against him so quickly that she could not have protested, had she wanted to. His lips covered hers as he sought to exorcise both his frustration and his escalating desire once and for all. He tugged Kara's head back, his mouth hard and unyielding as it demanded a response from her.

Her first thought was to resist Adam's sudden assault, but before her fevered mind could relay instructions to her body, her blood began to burn, her head began to swim and her lips, as if possessing a will of their own, opened desperately, hungrily, under his.

His wide fingers clasped the back of her head as he captured her lips in a devastating kiss that made her feel as if the wildly spinning world had just tilted on its axis. As Kara willingly gave herself up to the power of Adam's kiss, she experienced a hunger of her own that was like nothing she had ever known. She met him eagerly, passion for passion, unashamed of the primitiveness of their shared need.

"I want you, Kara," he moaned against her hair. "More than I've ever wanted any woman in my life."

"I want you, too, Adam," she said softly.

Below them, the surf beat against the lava rocks crowding the narrow white beach, as it had for millions of years. The cry of seabirds, diving for fish, filled the plumeria-scented air, and mingled with the carefree laughter of children frolicking in the playground adjacent to the small library building. But it was Kara's gentle rippling sigh that captured Adam's attention.

He took a deep breath, waiting for his voice to regain its usual steady tone. "Why do I hear a *but* in that declaration?"

Slipping out of his embrace, Kara made her way to the edge of the cliff and stood looking out over the water. He wanted to go to her, to touch her, but something in the resolute way she had squared her shoulders stopped him. He slipped his hands into his pockets and waited.

He shouldn't feel so good, Kara thought as she watched the silver splash of a family of dolphins playing offshore. Shouldn't taste so good. But he did, and heaven help her, she was so very, very tempted.

"I promised Liz I'd spend the evening with her," she said, spinning around to meet his outwardly patient stare head-on. "Whether you believe it or not, she's very upset about Brett's disappearance. She shouldn't be alone at a time like this."

Adam's eyes skimmed her face. "That's all right; I've got to go to Oahu," he said mildly.

Having expected a determined, persuasive argument, Kara was suspicious of his acquiescent tone. "Oahu? Why?"

When another woman came instantly to mind, Kara recognized in herself a feeling close to jealousy and quickly discarded it as ridiculous. She had no claims on Adam Lassiter. What business was it of hers how he spent his time? Or who he spent it with.

"Because I promised to help your friend," he answered simply. "And since she won't make things easier by telling me the truth, I've decided to do a little digging."

Gratitude suddenly filled Kara's somber gray eyes. "Thank you, Adam. Liz's happiness means a lot to me."

He crossed the expanse of flower-dotted meadow grass between them and ran his palm down her hair. "Don't think this little reprieve gets you off the hook," he warned with a smile. "A lovely woman once suggested that I learn to follow my instincts, to act on my impulses." His tone was like silk, flowing over her, wrapping her in its soft, enticing folds. "After giving the matter a great deal of study and consideration, I decided to take her up on it."

He bent his head and brushed his smiling mouth against hers, punctuating his words with delicate little kisses. "God, I'm going to miss you while I'm on Oahu."

"I'm going to miss you, too," she admitted as she found herself responding to the butterfly-soft kisses.

"Want to forget about Liz and Brett and spend the evening making love in your brother's passion pit?" He plucked at her lower lip with his teeth, rewarded as he felt her regretful little sigh against his mouth. Her soft, sweet breath was like a gentle summer breeze.

"Don't tempt me."

"Why not? That's what you've been doing since you practically attacked me on the beach walking home from your father's unveiling."

"Me? Attack you?" She slipped out of his arms and began gathering up the scattered books. "You certainly have a selective memory, Captain Lassiter," she said as she brushed past him, heading through the field of yellow flowers toward the small frame building that housed the library.

With his long stride, Adam caught up with her easily. "Okay, perhaps it was mutual. But I certainly don't remember either one of us complaining." He grinned, a wide, boyish grin that struck at something elemental deep within her. "And I am spending my valuable vacation time helping out your friend," he reminded her. "The least you could do is show your appreciation."

The smile that had been teasing now blossomed full-blown, and Kara laughed with reluctant good humor. "You're going to drive me crazy, Captain."

Adam planted a firm, noisy kiss on her tilted lips. "I'm certainly going to try."

8

USING WILLPOWER she had not been aware of possessing, Kara forced herself to keep her mind on her work as she spent the rest of the afternoon researching topics that ranged from movie trivia to famous sea battles to the unlikely subject of fabulous feasts throughout history. Kara was well aware that her chosen occupation was not taken seriously by a majority of educated, high-minded people. Personally, she couldn't think of anything that suited her more.

The simple truth of the matter was that Kara had always been enamored of education for education's sake. She had not, like so many of her contemporaries, gone off to college with a profession in mind. Instead, she had drifted through the system, changing majors with frequency, gathering up degrees with the same enjoyable abandon as she plucked flowers from her free-form rock garden.

She supposed she could have drifted on like that forever, had fate not stepped in during one of her infrequent visits to her brother in California. Colin's latest novel was in the process of being made into a movie, and despite his innate distaste for the film industry, Colin had thought Kara would enjoy spending a day or two on the set.

While visiting the set, Kara was taken on a tour of the Century City studio, which was also the home of several television programs. It had been there she had witnessed the taping of a popular game show and met the producer. When asked how she had enjoyed the show, Kara had offered a hesitant opinion that the audience, as well as the contestants, were capable of enjoying a wider range of questions. Questions that required additional thought, more depth.

To Kara's astonishment, Jeffrey Marshall invited her to submit some sample questions. She had, the staff had tested them on nearly one hundred hopeful contestants, and if she had had the good sense to stop there, everything would have been perfect.

But Kara, in an effort to rise to the exalted heights of her family's achievements, threw herself into her work in a way that now, five years later, she could only describe as obsessive. It hadn't been enough to merely write thoughtful, interesting questions. No, Kara had decided that she would be considered more successful if she were a producer.

After six months, she was fully responsible for a popular television quiz show; within a year, she was producing three current affairs shows and developing ideas for future ones. She was not the first Tiernan to make it in Hollywood; Maggie, of course, had achieved stellar status. But about the same time one of her suggestions had become a hit new show, Kara realized that she was dangerously close to a Tiernan family first: a nervous breakdown.

It was then she had returned to the island. For the past five years, since she had returned to writing questions, she had been in seventh heaven, earning her living uncovering little-known facts about a myriad of disparate topics. After her near-disaster, she had learned not to care what others thought of her admittedly strange profession.

Until Adam, she was forced to admit as she drove down the dirt road toward Liz's beachfront house early that evening. For some undiscernible reason, it had been vastly important that he not belittle her work.

"SO WHAT'S THE STORY with the hunk?"
Kara took a sip of the mai tai Liz had mixed for them af-

ter dinner. "And here I thought you were going out of your mind with worry over Brett," she hedged smoothly.

"I am. But that doesn't mean that I don't care about my best friend's love life."

"Adam's only here on vacation; he'll be going back to the mainland."

"That's what he says now; I've known more than one mainland type to get hooked on the islands. Look at Brett." With that, her lovely green eyes grew misty and Liz turned away, staring out over the moon-silvered water. "I'm so worried about him, Kara." When she returned her gaze to Kara's, her expression was more earnest than her friend had ever seen it. "Your Adam will be able to find Brett, won't he? He is as good as you say he is?"

"He's not my Adam," Kara corrected absently. Try as she might, she had not been able to get Adam's allegation about Liz out of her mind. "But Colin says he's the best. And he wouldn't be being considered for police chief if he wasn't very, very good at his work."

She put her glass down on the table and leaned forward, her hands pressed together, her short square nails digging into the skin. "Liz," Kara prompted gently, "did you tell Adam everything you know about Brett's disappearance?"

Something like desperation flashed in Liz's eyes but was gone before Kara could fully comprehend its meaning. "Of course I did."

Reaching out, Kara took one of Liz's hands in hers. It was ice-cold. "Are you certain that you didn't leave something out? Something that perhaps slipped your mind at the time?"

Jerking her hand free, Liz crossed the room and pulled a pack of menthol cigarettes from her straw bag. As she lit the cigarette, her hands were trembling visibly. "Really, Kara," she insisted firmly, "I think you've been spending too much time with that cop. Since when do you cross-examine your best friend?"

"You're right," Kara said with a forced smile. "Let's talk about something else. Have you seen the new show at the Artisans' Guild in Hanalei?"

Kara knew when she was licked. She also knew that Adam had been right: Liz was lying. But what was she hiding? And why?

KARA WAS ON HER KNEES, applying mastic to the back of a piece of smooth, ivory ceramic tile when she felt someone watching her. Already knowing who it would be, she made an attempt to stay calm but wasn't able to, and lifted her eyes. The hand she had lifted to rub the back of her weary neck dropped to her side.

"You're back." *Great opening line,* she railed inwardly as she tried to stop the welcoming smile from blossoming on her lips.

"I'm back."

There was an uncomfortable little silence as they looked at each other. Just when Kara thought that Adam was going to say something intimate, perhaps even profound, his warm blue eyes swept across the bathroom.

"You're right."

"Right?"

Her throat was dry; her lips felt like bricks. With an impatience she was unaccustomed to feeling, Kara had been waiting anxiously, almost desperately, for this moment. Now that it had arrived, her brain seemed to have turned to scrambled eggs. To add to Kara's intense discomfort, Adam appeared to be no more comfortable than she with the situation.

"The tile," he mumbled. "I like it."

The more
you love romance . . .
the more
you'll love this offer

FREE!

Mail this heart today! (See inside)

**Join us on a Harlequin Honeymoon
and we'll give you
4 free books
A free makeup mirror and brush kit
And a free mystery gift**

IT'S A
HARLEQUIN HONEYMOON—
A SWEETHEART
OF A FREE OFFER!
HERE'S WHAT YOU GET:

1. **Four New Harlequin Temptation® Novels—FREE!**
   Take a Harlequin Honeymoon with your four exciting
   romances—yours FREE from Harlequin Reader Service. Each of
   these hot-off-the-press novels brings you the passion and tenderness of today's greatest love stories...your free passports to bright
   new worlds of love and foreign adventure.

2. **A Lighted Makeup Mirror and Brush
   Kit—FREE!**
   This lighted makeup mirror and brush kit al-
   lows plenty of light for those quick touch-ups.
   It operates on two easy-to-replace batteries and
   bulbs (batteries not included). It holds everything you need for a perfect finished look yet is
   small enough to slip into your purse or pocket—
   4-⅛" x 3" closed.

3. **An Exciting Mystery Bonus—FREE!**
   You'll be thrilled with this surprise gift. It will be the source of
   many compliments, as well as a useful and attractive addition to
   your home.

4. **Money-Saving Home Delivery!**
   Join Harlequin Reader Service and enjoy the convenience of pre-
   viewing four new books every month delivered right to your home.
   Each book is yours for only $2.24—26¢ less per book than what
   you pay in stores. And there is no extra charge for postage and
   handling. Great savings plus total convenience add up to a sweetheart of a deal for you!

5. **Free Newsletter**
   It's *heart to heart*, the indispensable insider's look at our most
   popular writers, upcoming books, even recipes from your favorite authors.

6. **More Surprise Gifts**
   Because our home subscribers are our most valued readers, we'll
   be sending you additional free gifts from time to time—as a token
   of our appreciation.

   START YOUR HARLEQUIN HONEYMOON TODAY—JUST
   COMPLETE, DETACH AND MAIL YOUR FREE-OFFER CARD

Get your fabulous gifts
ABSOLUTELY FREE!

MAIL THIS CARD TODAY.

GIVE YOUR HEART TO HARLEQUIN

YES! Please send me my four Harlequin Temptation novels FREE, along with my free lighted makeup mirror and brush kit and free mystery gift as explained on the opposite page.

PLACE
HEART STICKER
HERE

NAME _____
(PLEASE PRINT)

ADDRESS _____ APT. ____

CITY _____ STATE _____

ZIP CODE _____ 142 CIH MDPG

HARLEQUIN READER SERVICE "NO RISK" GUARANTEE

— There's no obligation to buy—and the free books and gifts remain yours to keep.
— You pay the lowest price possible and receive books before they appear in stores.
— You may end your subscription anytime—just write and let us know.

PRINTED IN U.S.A.

START YOUR
HARLEQUIN HONEYMOON TODAY.
JUST COMPLETE, DETACH AND MAIL YOUR
FREE OFFER CARD.

If offer card below is missing, write to: Harlequin Reader Service, 901 Fuhrmann Blvd.
P.O. Box 1394, Buffalo, NY, 14240-1394

BUSINESS REPLY CARD

First Class   Permit No. 717   Buffalo, NY

Postage will be paid by addressee

Harlequin Reader Service®
901 Fuhrmann Blvd.
P.O. Box 1394
Buffalo, NY 14240-9963

NO POSTAGE
NECESSARY
IF MAILED
IN THE
UNITED STATES

"Oh."

"I've been meaning to ask you, where did you learn to do all this?" His smile was slightly off center and vaguely self-conscious. "I've never known a lady handyman."

"Makaio Kuala taught me."

"Oh?"

The tension in the air was beginning to make her head throb. "He lives next door to my parents. I sort of grew up over there," she explained. "The members of my family were always locked away in their various studios, being ultracreative—Daddy with his horrible paintings, Mother with her sculptures, Colin with his stories—so, feeling like a fifth wheel a lot, I used to go visit Makaio. He's a local contractor; he built all our houses—my parents', this one, mine. I'm certainly not in his league, but he taught me everything I know."

"I see."

Kara wondered if the sharp edge in his voice could possibly be born of jealousy. "He's seventy-one years old," she offered. "And still working."

Adam had to struggle to keep from revealing his relief. He hadn't liked the idea of Kara spending all her time with this Makaio fellow. Especially when his mind had conjured up an image of one of those bronzed beachboys who inhabited the islands.

"Good for old Makaio," he said.

Once again they fell silent. Adam leaned against the doorframe, his hands jammed into the pockets of the dress slacks he had worn on the plane. Kara returned to the task of cutting the tile, but her fingers were suddenly unsteady.

"Damn." The blade slipped, leaving a gash across the tip of her index finger. Kara immediately stuck her finger in her mouth.

He was by her side in seconds, lifting her to her feet. "Here, let me."

Kara didn't argue as she sat on the edge of the deep, circular bathtub, complete with Jacuzzi, that she had installed at Colin's request, and allowed Adam to apply the bandage to the cut, which though not deep, had begun to bleed. When he appeared in no hurry to release her hand, Kara wondered if he could feel her trembling.

Adam looked down into her smoky eyes and willed himself to remain calm. Over the years he had come to think of himself as a rock—unemotional, immovable. Somehow, during their short time together, and even more during the time he had spent on Oahu, Adam had learned a great deal about himself. The first and foremost thing was that he was a hell of a long way away from being the self-controlled, impervious man he had worked so hard to become.

Go with your instincts. He had to remind himself of what he had been vowing to do for the past twenty-four hours.

"Do you have any idea how hard it was to keep my mind on Liz's errant boyfriend while I was away from you?" His fingers trailed lazily over her face. "Any idea at all?"

Kara's eyes widened at Adam's husky tone, at the touch of hands that, like her own, were anything but steady. As she was pulled into the stormy blue sea of his eyes, Kara didn't even care that she could easily drown in those swirling depths.

"Speaking of Brett, did you learn anything about his disappearance?"

"Not exactly, but I found out something rather curious about Liz's little visits to Oahu," he murmured as he idly wrapped a long coppery strand of her hair around his finger.

"What?"

He bent his head, burying it in a handful of thick, fragrant hair. "What business do you think Liz would have with the FBI?"

"FBI? Liz's been meeting with the FBI?" Although Kara had realized last night that Liz had been keeping something from her, never in a million years would she have expected the FBI to be that something.

"On at least two occasions that I know about." His lips trailed around her ear, thrilling her in a way that made coherent thought increasingly difficult. "Kara?"

"Yes, Adam?"

"Is there any chance we could talk about Liz a little later?"

Desire overruled curiosity as Kara twined her arms around his neck and tangled her fingers in the sun-gilded strands of his hair. "Later," she agreed softly.

The light of victory blazed in Adam's dark eyes. Kara's soft admission was all the invitation he needed. He scooped her into his arms and carried her into the bedroom.

"Damn," Kara murmured as Adam placed her on the bed. The frankly fake fur was soft and lush against the back of her legs.

Adam frowned. "What's the matter?"

Kara's smile was warm and unashamedly sensual. "I hate it when Colin's right."

Adam's answering chuckle came from deep in his throat. "You had me scared there for a minute," he said as he nuzzled her ear. "I thought you'd changed your mind."

"I have. A million times," she admitted, weakening as his fingers trailed lazily up the exposed length of her suntanned thigh.

"And?"

"And I keep coming back to the fact that I want you."

"Good." His self-satisfied smile should have irritated her, but didn't. "Because I've wanted you from the beginning.

You've been all I could think about from the first moment I saw you, with the sun striking sparks in your hair. If you'd been looking closely, you would have known what a man looks like when he's been hit by lightning."

Kara stroked his cheek. "I felt the same way."

He framed her face in his hands. "And now?"

"I wonder why we waited this long."

Adam's taste, as he covered her lips with his, was warm, mysterious, tinged with something undefinably male. It filled her head, leaving room for little else. His skin was rough with a day's growth of beard, but as he tilted his head, changing the angle of the kiss, Kara shivered, excited, as it grazed her face in a strangely erotic way.

As his fingers toyed with the buttons of her pink gauze blouse, Adam experienced an almost staggering sense of relief when he saw Kara's eyes warm with the unmistakable heat of desire. Pushing the material aside, he drew in a breath at the sight of her smooth, golden skin. The globed softness of her breasts strained against the barrier of lacy pink net, the areolae surrounding the nipples gleaming a deep, dusky rose. When his palm covered the feminine scrap of lace, Kara's breasts swelled to fit his hand, creating a responding stir in Adam's loins.

"Your skin feels like the underside of a flower petal," he murmured, his lips brushing slowly across her tingling breasts. "Roses," he decided as his tongue swirled around their dark circles. "Soft, lush, velvet. And sweet. So very, very sweet."

His teeth tugged at first one taut, rosy bud and then the other, stimulating them to a pleasure just this side of pain before he returned his mouth to hers, his lips brushing teasingly, tantalizingly against hers. Adam could feel Kara melting under his touch, and the idea that he could make her weak with just his hands, his mouth, was vastly pleasing.

Despite the urging of his body to take her then, quickly, Adam luxuriated in the feel of her fluid body as it moved under his hands, delighted in her soft sighs that filled his mouth and took his time to savor the way her body trembled as he ran his strong fingers up and down the silky flesh of her thighs.

When his fingers toyed with the button on her shorts, then moved tantalizingly away, Kara caught his hand. "Oh, please," she whispered, lifting her hips off the mattress to press against that wicked, clever hand. "Please, Adam."

Kara was beyond caring that what she was doing was begging. His taste—dark, warm, and wonderfully, masculinely musky—had filled her head. His touch, as his hands ran over her body, promising untold delights, made her skin hum as if he'd touched a live wire to her flesh.

"Anything to oblige a lady." He whisked the garment off her with a speed that had her practically shuddering with relief. Now, she assured her flaming body. Now it would finally receive satisfaction.

After quickly divesting her of the cotton barrier between them, Adam settled back into his slow, achingly seductive lovemaking. His fingers trailed leisurely up and down her legs, creating sparks wherever they lingered. When they slipped under the elastic leg band of her silky pink panties, tugging at the soft red curls at the juncture of her thighs, Kara moaned.

Intrigued, Adam repeated the intimate gesture, this time covering Kara's parted lips with his in order to feel her ragged moan as well as hear it.

"I love you like this," he said against her mouth. As one hand teased the silken strands, the other slid down past her waistband, his fingers cupping her derriere possessively. "Warm, loving, holding nothing back."

His palms pressed against the glowing flesh of her inner thighs. "Open for me, sweetheart," he instructed huskily. "I want to know that you need me as much as I need you."

"I do," Kara whispered without shame or embarrassment as she did as Adam asked. She was beyond such feelings; all that existed was this shimmering, ethereal moment. She could no longer tell where her heated flesh left off and the soft fur on which she lay began.

"Oh, my God," she cried out, as he pressed his lips against the silky material of her panties. His breath warmed her already-flaming skin, creating a desire that she could no longer control.

Fueled by her rising need, Kara felt her sensual, almost languid weakness replaced by a strength she had not known she possessed. Slipping from his gentle hold, she rose up on her knees to free him from the blue silk tie around his neck.

"City clothes," she muttered disparagingly, tossing the tie across the room, where it landed on a bamboo chaise. "They have to go." A moment later the crisp white shirt followed.

The bronze glow of his chest, gleaming in the golden light of early evening, enthralled Kara. She trailed her fingers along the broad line of his shoulders, pressed her palms against the inviting tawny skin of his lean torso. When she touched her lips to his warm, moist flesh, Kara imagined she could actually taste the wild pounding of his heart.

Reality was rapidly slipping away as they finished undressing each other. Lying diagonally across the soft plush of the bed, they refused to rush, as if by unspoken agreement. His hands explored her body, learning every soft dip, each gentle curve. In turn, Kara discovered fluid muscle and steely strength. Wherever his long dark fingers lingered, she flamed; wherever her slender hands played, he burned.

Outside the cottage the brilliant twilight colors of the sky bled together, drowning them in a shower of golden warmth. The pace quickened; hands that were once content to loiter now moved more urgently. Soft sighs became husky moans. Tender kisses became eager, hungry. Patience grew difficult, control impossible as reason slipped away, and they were guided by sense alone into a swirling inferno where passion ruled and desire became a primitive, almost savage, thing.

Unable to do anything else, they clung to each other. As they joined, Kara's last coherent thought was that the twilight seemed to light and glow with fire all its own. Then there were no more thoughts.

HAD IT BEEN HOURS, or only minutes? Days or an eternity? Kara lay in Adam's arms as she struggled to orient herself. The warm, fiery glow of sunset had melted into yawning shadows that created soft blue silhouettes on the walls.

Outside the open window, all was quiet as the birds settled down for the night. The only sounds were the rustle of palm fronds disturbed by the gentle trade winds and the soft sigh of the tide as it washed delicate shells onto the coral beach.

"Well," she said, arching her back like a lithe, pampered cat, "I surrender."

Adam ran his hand lazily down her side. "I thought you already had." There was no mistaking the pleased smile in his voice.

"I was talking about the fact that any man who can make me feel the way you do could probably make me confess to anything. No wonder you're so good at your work, Adam."

He brushed a few strands of still-damp hair off her forehead and pressed his lips against her temple. "It's only been that way with you, Kara," he said truthfully.

Kara laughed as she turned in the circle of his arms and tangled her legs with his long hair-roughened ones. "Really?" she asked with a coy look that Scarlett O'Hara would have envied.

It was not in Kara's nature to flirt so outrageously, but since she would freely admit to having acted a great deal out of character lately, she wasn't going to let that stop her from enjoying this delicious aftermath of passion.

"Really." His lips nibbled at hers as he punctuated his words with soft, teasing kisses. "I've never met a woman who can make me lose control the way you do."

"I think I like the idea of making you lose control," she murmured silkily, as she trailed a slow, lazy finger up his inner thigh.

"Kara . . ."

Adam closed his eyes, gathering strength as he felt desire returning with a fury that he would have thought impossible, given the force of their earlier lovemaking. His hard-won self-restraint was too delicately balanced, and as a man used to maintaining control over all aspects of his life, Adam found what Kara was capable of doing to both his mind and his body undeniably intriguing and just a little frightening.

"Yes?" she asked prettily, and then her lips pressed against his throat.

Adam took her hand and held it against the straining proof of his arousal. "I think," he said as he gave her a long, blissful kiss, "that you're making me crazy again."

Kara's answering laughter was light and breathless. "You've got no idea how happy I am to hear that," she said, as she drew him inside her. "Let's be crazy together."

THE ENTIRE EASTERN ARC of the horizon danced with fire as Adam rose to greet the new day. A day, he had considered on first awakening, that was filled with possibilities. After the previous night, he felt himself imbued with almost mystical powers; whatever he wished for would be his; whatever he sought, he would find. Life was his oyster, Kara his pearl and everything was coming up roses.

He laughed as he realized that he'd slipped from waxing philosophical into mixing metaphors. Both were admittedly uncommon behavior for him, but this was a remarkably uncommon day. Even waking to an empty bed couldn't diminish his optimistic mood, because Adam had a pretty good hunch exactly where Kara was.

Wandering out onto the lanai, a cup of coffee in his hand, he saw her. She was strolling along the slender crescent of glistening sand, picking up the shells that littered the shoreline. The sea, illuminated by the rising sun, gleamed like molten metal almost too bright to look at.

Ah, but Kara was a different matter entirely, Adam thought, his lips curving in an instinctive smile as he watched her pick up a shell, turn it over in her hand as she studied it intently, only to discard it. He could happily spend the rest of his life watching his lovely Kara do anything. Or nothing. He was so entranced by her that Adam felt as if she were a mythical Lorelei and he nothing more than a bewitched sailor.

As if sensing his eyes on her, Kara looked up. It wasn't until she smiled and waved that Adam realized he had been holding his breath. Adam had known full well that he was going to spend last night with Kara wrapped in his arms. He had decided while on Oahu that he was going to make love to her as soon as he returned to the island.

What he hadn't entirely thought out was the possibility of everything falling apart the following morning. Adam recognized this uncharacteristic act as yet another departure from his usual prudent behavior. Captain Adam Lassiter was renowned for his propensity to look at a question—any question, no matter how grave or how trivial—from all sides.

"Go with your instincts," Kara had told him. Well, he had certainly done that. And so far he wasn't regretting a single moment.

"Hi," Kara said a little breathlessly as she came up the wooden steps. "I couldn't sleep. But I didn't want to wake you."

"I wouldn't have minded."

His warm gaze triggered thoughts of last night's lovemaking. Neither of them had shown any compunction about waking the other. In vain Kara tried to remember exactly how many times they had turned to each other in the deep ebony darkness.

Scattering her seashells on a nearby table, she framed his smiling face in her palms. "Ah, but I didn't want to wear you out."

He pulled her against him with one arm. "Think that's possible?"

His rough, challenging tone thrilled her. Kara linked her fingers around the back of his neck and allowed herself to drown in his kiss.

"No," she said finally, when she had found her voice. "In fact, if word of your stamina ever leaks out, you can say goodbye to your police career, Adam."

She glanced down at the cup he still held in his free hand. Steam rose invitingly into the tropical morning air, and the rich fragrance of the dark Kona coffee was enticing. "What are my chances of getting a cup of that?"

"After last night, you can have anything your warm little heart desires," he admitted, releasing her to return to the kitchen. "What do you mean, my career would be shot?" he asked as he poured her a cup of the fragrant brew.

"Thanks." She took a tentative sip of the too-hot coffee before dumping in her extra ration of sugar. "I was referring to all those scientists who'd track you down and lock you away in some laboratory while they sought to find the secret of your amazing virility."

Her gray eyes danced as she grinned up at him. "If we could find a way to bottle whatever keeps you going, Captain, we'd make a fortune."

He snapped his fingers. "No problem. The answer is simple." As his gaze turned suddenly dark, Kara felt an answering warmth curling outward to her fingertips.

"It's you, Kara," he said with a strange, unnerving solemnity. "Only you."

Unfortunately, it wasn't simple at all, Kara thought ruefully, as she was forced to admit that Adam appeared to be telling the truth. Kara was not a promiscuous woman, but she was experienced enough to know that something as rare as it was beautiful had passed between them last night, something that if the circumstances were different would have her shouting her love to the rooftops. Simple? Hardly.

"Were you telling the truth?" she asked suddenly.

Adam's eyes narrowed at Kara's quiet, oddly desperate tone. He forced his expression into a calm he no longer felt. "About what?" he asked, congratulating himself on his steady voice.

Kara dragged her gaze away from those suddenly intent blue eyes. "About not wanting to get married," she mumbled, staring at a smudge on the chrome handle of the refrigerator.

Under normal circumstances, Adam would have automatically read Kara's words as a plea for some promise of commitment or permanency. Such thoughts were certainly acceptable after a night of lovemaking. He had learned a long time ago that women often wanted to hear the words, even if they didn't have any real desire to settle down themselves. The words themselves seemed to be enough to assure them that the night had been special. That they were special.

The strange thing was, Adam mused, observing her oddly pale face, that if he didn't know better, he'd think Kara was begging him to assure her that this was nothing more than a one-night stand. No, not that, he corrected thoughtfully. A vacation fling. A brief affair that would last only as long as his stay here on the island. He found that idea oddly distasteful.

When he realized Kara was still waiting for an answer, Adam did what any prudent man would do under similar circumstances. He hedged.

"I didn't come down here looking for a wife, if that's what you mean."

That was what she had wanted to hear, wasn't it, Kara reminded herself. So why did his words make her feel so rotten?

"Good," she said, nodding her head in counterfeit satisfaction. "I just thought we should clear up any misunderstandings that might have occurred after last night."

At her smooth, casual tone, Adam was struck with the dual impulses to grind his teeth and shake Kara senseless. In the end he did neither.

"I take it you're still dead set against the institution of matrimony."

"Absolutely." She heard a strong, firm voice and marveled that it could possibly be her own.

For some reason Kara's firmly issued declaration grated on him. Unwilling to pursue the cause, Adam decided the time had come to turn the conversation back to a more enjoyable track.

"Hungry?" he asked.

"Famished," she agreed with a smile that only wobbled slightly.

"Were you serious about Liz meeting with the FBI?" Kara asked as they sat out on the lanai, eating a breakfast of banana bread and fresh fruit.

"I wouldn't kid about a thing like that."

She shook her head. "It has to be a mistake."

"I'm not mistaken, Kara. I've found two taxi drivers who took her there and another who picked her up."

"They could be mistaken."

"Honey, in case you haven't noticed, your friend isn't exactly the type of woman the average man could easily mistake for anyone else. Besides, hair that blond definitely stands out here in the islands."

"But what would she be doing at the FBI?"

He shrugged. "I figured we'd ask her that. After breakfast."

As puzzled as she was by Liz's apparent subterfuge, Kara was excited by the idea of accompanying Adam on his investigation.

"You're letting me come with you?"

"After last night, I think I want to keep you close by. In case I get lonely again."

Kara smiled. "What a nice thing to say." She sipped her coffee, basking in the memory of being so thoroughly, expertly, loved. Adam's lovemaking had been every bit as intense as the man she remembered him to be before he had begun his successful series of career advancements. "Why do you want to be police chief?"

"It's the next logical step."

She frowned as she spread some orange marmalade on a thin slice of the warm, dark bread. "What exactly does a police chief do?"

"About what I do now," he said. "Only more of it.... Have I told you that you are absolutely beautiful this morning?"

She jerked her head back. "Damn it, Adam, I'm trying to have a serious conversation with you."

Adam regarded her squarely. "I can see you are," he said calmly. "So carry on."

"All right," Kara continued. "Why did you want to become a policeman in the first place?"

It had been so long since anyone had asked him that question that Adam had to stop and remember what had made him turn down a very lucrative offer from a Silicon Valley electronics firm after graduating from college in order to enter the police academy.

He leaned forward, bracing his elbows on the table as he considered her words. As she waited for her answer, Kara found herself suddenly restless without really knowing why.

"It's going to sound like braggadocio," he warned after a moment.

"Try me."

"I thought I could make a difference. That I could make the world, or at least my little part of it, a better place for people to live."

"And have you?" she asked, sipping at her coffee.

He leaned toward her, his eyes gleaming with a vaguely familiar light. It was the same light Kara had seen in Colin's crystal-blue eyes when her brother discussed his latest novel. She had also noticed it in her father's eyes when he was in the planning stages of a painting, and her mother had been known to have the same avid look while chiseling away on a piece of virgin marble. Able to recognize obsession when she saw it, Kara stifled a soft sigh.

"If I haven't, it hasn't been for lack of trying."

Kara believed him. There was still one little point she didn't understand. "When was the last time you actually talked with one of those people you wanted to help?" she asked quietly.

A puzzled frown darkened his brow. "I don't understand what you're getting at."

"I just was wondering if you'd ever have time to mingle with the masses once you become chief of police?"

He studied her thoughtfully. "Why am I getting the feeling that you disapprove of this promotion?"

Kara shrugged. "It's not for me to disapprove, Adam. I have nothing to say about what you do with your life."

Adam frowned. "That's what Marilyn used to say," he said. "Right before she pointed out all the disadvantages of being an ordinary street cop."

Stunned by the intrusion of another woman into the conversation, Kara picked up her mug, staring into the dark brown depths as if the cooling liquid held inordinate interest for her.

"Marilyn?"

His next words sent a knife through her heart. "My wife. Ex-wife," he corrected.

Kara had to ask. "How long have you been divorced?"

Adam didn't want to talk about Marilyn. Just thinking about his former wife gave him a sour taste in his mouth. "Eight years, but it seems like a lifetime," he murmured.

Lifting her wrist to his smiling lips, he pressed a soft kiss against her fragrant skin. "You taste so good," he said huskily. "I don't think I'm ever going to get enough of you."

The way he was looking at her made her pulse miss a beat. "Come back with me, Kara," he said suddenly. The moment he heard the impulsive suggestion escape his lips, Adam realized with a start that it sounded eminently agreeable. "You've shown me your island; let me show you my city by the bay."

The invitation was unmistakable and, Kara admitted bleakly, seemingly sincere. How could she explain that she couldn't go back to the mainland? Not even for him.

"Adam—" She began her refusal tentatively.

He bent his head, covering her mouth with his. "I know," he said, his reluctant sigh like a warm breeze against her lips, "I'm rushing things again."

His hands moved restlessly up and down her arms. "I've been trying to slow down to island speed, Kara, but when I'm with you, all I want to do is sweep you away somewhere where the world can never find us and we can spend the rest of our lives making mad, passionate love."

He made it sound like paradise. Heaven. Nirvana. It took every bit of Kara's willpower to resist the silent appeal in those warm blue eyes.

"I don't think anyone would be willing to pay us to do that," she protested lightly. "How would we eat?"

He ran his broad hands down her back and desire raced up her spine. "This is the Garden Island, remember? We'll live off the land; I'll fish in the morning and we'll spend the lazy, sun-filled days feeding each other sweet, succulent fruit. Passion fruit," he added significantly.

"I don't know if that's a very good idea," she protested. "Don't forget what happened to Adam and Eve."

"So we'll skip the apples."

"Still," Kara murmured, "I'm absolutely useless until I have my coffee in the morning. With milk. And sugar," she reminded him.

Adam refused to be deterred from his romantic fantasy. "I'll cash in my policeman's pension to buy you a warehouse of coffee and sugar. And a cow for the milk," he decided.

"But we'd have to tell them where to send your pension check and then they'd all find us—your police department, the mayor, my family—"

"You've made your point."

As he ran his hand over her hair, Adam couldn't quite banish the impulse to fling her over his shoulder caveman-style, and take her away where they could discover each other's secrets without any interference from the outside world. What secrets was Kara hiding from him, he wondered with concealed frustration. He knew she had them: they were continually rising, like some dark, forbidding wall between them, whenever things threatened to become too intimate.

No, Adam reflected, studying the problem with analytical precision, that wasn't actually the case. Last night had left no doubt as to Kara's willingness for intimacy. It was the future, he mused. Whenever talk turned to a relationship beyond this golden moment, she'd hide behind those daunting parapets.

Secrets. He vowed that before his time with her was over, he would not only know every last one of Kara Tiernan's private monsters, but he would have managed to convince her that they were nothing but paper demons.

"Let's get this business with Liz out of the way," he said suddenly, fighting against instincts that were growing stronger by the minute.

"All right. And then I can come back here and finish the tile in the bathroom. And, if I have time, patch your roof."

"Uh-uh." He waved away her plans with a flick of his wrist. "I seem to have been struck with the aloha spirit; I want to spend the day playing with my lady."

Kara couldn't think of anything she'd rather do. "What if it rains? If I recall, you were worried about your roof leaking."

He shrugged uncaringly. "I've got that little problem all solved."

She lifted a russet brow. "Don't tell me that *you're* going to fix the roof?"

"Of course not; if there's one thing my work has taught me to be, it's a good administrator. And a good administrator always delegates."

"Delegates?"

He nodded, the expression on his handsome face smug. "If it rains while we're making love," he explained, "I'm delegating you to the top position."

"Gee, thanks," she drawled.

He pressed his hand against the back of her head, pulling her forward for an intense, explosive kiss. Stars glittered and spun on a backdrop of black velvet behind Kara's eyes, and she could have sworn she felt the distant rumbling of Mount Waialeale. But that was impossible, she told herself as her hands clutched Adam's shoulder tightly. The volcano that had once served as Pele's home was now extinct; the goddess of fire had long since moved to other islands.

"Wow," Kara murmured, tilting her head back to stare into his storm-filled blue eyes. "I think I feel an earthquake coming on."

"I feel it, too," Adam agreed with a slow, inviting smile. "And I'm willing to bet it's about to go off the Richter scale all over the islands." He stood up, holding out his hand. "Come to bed with me, Kara."

"But what about Liz?" she asked reluctantly. "Shouldn't we be interrogating her, or whatever it is you call asking her why she lied?"

"Since when did you get so practical?" he responded, a note of frustration in his voice.

"If we're going to find Brett, one of us has to be."

"I suppose so," he complained dryly. "But who would ever have expected it to be you?" He pushed himself out of the chair. "Come on, honey, let's get the business part of the day out of the way so we can get on with the pleasure."

Honey. Even as the easily spoken endearment warmed her to the core, Kara reminded herself that it was, after all, a fairly impersonal word. Waitresses used it regularly. So did hairdressers. Not to mention Mrs. Kekupaa down at the market. It wasn't any big deal.

Even so, try as she might, Kara couldn't quite wipe the satisfied smile off her face. It remained on her lips during the entire drive to Liz's and Brett's conveniently adjoining shops.

9

KARA AND ADAM found Liz sitting in the midst of what could charitably be called a mess. It looked as though a hurricane had gone through Pacific Paradise Adventures.

Boxes of equipment had been slashed open and masks, snorkels and tanks tossed carelessly aside. The usually well-stocked shelves were bare, their contents spread over the floor. A saltwater aquarium had been overturned; the gaily colored tropical fish lay lifeless among the wreckage. Brett's shop had been thoroughly, expertly ransacked.

"What on earth?" Kara stared in disbelief at the scene.

"It's no better next door," Liz moaned, jerking her head in the direction of the door that connected the two businesses. "It'll take me all day to clean up."

"What were they looking for, Liz?" Adam asked. From his calm expression, Kara got the impression that such vandalism was a routine event for him. All in a day's work. She marveled at his ability to remain composed when her own heart was beating like a jackhammer.

Liz's platinum hair skimmed her shoulders as she shook her head. "I don't know."

"Dammit." Adam squatted in front of her, grabbed her shoulders and gave her a firm shake. "Don't you realize this is getting serious? You could be in danger, Liz. The goons who tore this place apart could decide to come after you next. As soon as they realize that you know what Britton's been up to."

Liz's golden complexion went chalk white. "But I don't," she wailed. She turned accusing tear-filled eyes toward Kara. "You didn't tell me he was so mean."

Kara shot Adam a severe look. "Can't you see she's had a terrible shock?" She joined them amid the rubble on the floor and ran a calming hand down her friend's hair. "Liz," she coaxed softly, "what were you doing at the FBI offices?"

Liz's startled green eyes flew to Adam, seeking confirmation of Kara's words, but his expression remained inscrutable. "Oh, Kara," she said, "I wanted to tell you. But I was afraid you'd think that I'm a terrible person."

"Never," Kara declared at once.

"A few months ago," Liz began, "a man came into my shop to buy some candy for his kids. He said he was an FBI agent and had come to the island for a meeting with the local police. Anyway, he was friendly enough, although a bit formal for my usual taste, and in a kind of stiff, mainland way, good-looking." She glanced over at Adam. "Actually, now that I think about it, he reminded me a great deal of you, Adam."

"Thanks. I think," Adam returned dryly. "What did the guy want with you?"

"I told you," Liz insisted, "he simply came into the shop to buy some saltwater taffy. But it was a slow day and Brett had taken a two-day charter over to the Big Island, so I was grateful to have someone to talk to."

"What did you talk about?" Adam asked.

"Really, Adam," Liz protested, "that's a little personal."

"In case you haven't noticed, this vandalism has gotten a little personal," Adam pointed out. "So let's try it again; what did you two talk about?"

She glared at him. "Just the usual things men and women talk about when the man is trying to pick the woman up and the woman's trying to decide whether she's going to let him. Surely you've got a few tried-and-true lines of your own, Adam."

She paused for a moment. "Anyway, after a while, he asked me if I wanted to have a drink with him. Since I wasn't doing any business, I agreed. Of course that was my big mistake."

"Why?" Kara asked.

"Because I was attracted to him, that's why. Despite the fact that he was all wrong for me. For heaven's sake, Kara, haven't you ever been irresistibly drawn to a man against your better judgment?"

Kara could feel Adam's suddenly sharp eyes directed toward her face and steadfastly refused to look at him. "Of course I have," she mumbled. "Are you telling me that you had an affair with this man?"

Liz was twisting her hands together in her lap. "Oh, I knew it was foolish. He was married, after all. And I was engaged to Brett. After a few weeks I tried to break it off, but when I told him I wouldn't see him again, he threatened to tell Brett all about us." She buried her face in her hands. "I didn't know what to do. I knew I should confess the truth to Brett, but I was so afraid of how he'd react. He's so jealous."

"Do you think the man told Brett about the affair?" Kara asked. "Do you think that's why he left?"

"I don't know," Liz admitted. "I went over to Oahu yesterday to confront him with my suspicions, but he swore he hadn't said a word to Brett about us." Her slender shoulders slumped dejectedly. "I believed him."

"So," Adam said slowly, "I suppose that puts us right back where we started."

"I'm afraid so." Liz's expression was clearly apologetic. "There is one thing," she offered hesitantly.

By this point Adam had decided not to get his hopes up about anything Liz Forsythe might have to offer about her missing boyfriend. "What's that?"

"You might try the Blue Parrot. That's where Brett liked to hang out, when he wasn't on his boat or with me. It's in Nawiliwili, on the waterfront."

"It's worth a try," Adam said. "Let me know if the police find anything when they go over this place," he instructed Liz.

She paled visibly at his words. "Police?"

"You are going to call them, aren't you?"

Liz paused for the space of a heartbeat. It was a struggle, but she managed to regain her composure. "Of course."

Adam nodded brusquely. "Of course," he agreed dryly, taking Kara's elbow and leading her out of the shop. "I'll call you later, Liz. After I check out the bar."

Once outside, Adam put on the dark glasses he'd purchased to protect his eyes from the tropical glare. "For a woman supposedly unaccustomed to lying, your friend sure tells some whoppers," he muttered as they returned to the Jeep.

"What does that mean?"

"It means that she was no more having an illicit affair with the Fed than I was."

Kara's eyes narrowed as she looked up at him. His gaze was frustratingly enigmatic behind the lenses of the dark glasses. "How on earth did you come to that conclusion? Adam, it was obvious that Liz was horribly upset about the entire affair. For good reason."

"She's upset, granted. But not about any affair. That whole damned story was nothing but a smoke screen to keep us from finding out the real reason for her FBI connection."

"You can't know that for certain," Kara argued.

"I'd be willing to bet my pension on it," he retorted. "Believe me, Kara, after a while you get a gut feeling that tells you when a person's prevaricating, something your friend has been doing from the beginning."

"Couldn't you simply ask the FBI what she was doing there?"

Adam shook his head. "Not until we know what the hell is going on. She's your friend, Kara. I wouldn't want to be responsible for landing her in more trouble than she's already in."

He fell silent, and it was obvious that he was deep in thought. Kara forced herself to remain quiet as she impatiently awaited his next move. She was to have a long wait: nearly twenty minutes passed before Adam suddenly looked over at her.

"What's the name of the police chief on the island?" he asked as if there had been no break in the conversation.

"Manny Kanualu. Why?"

"I think I'll pay Chief Kanualu a little visit," Adam said, rubbing his jaw thoughtfully. "Professional courtesy, and all that. And afterward, I suppose I'd better check out the Blue Parrot. Not that I trust Liz to give us anything of substance."

"Oh, good. I've always wanted to see the inside of one of those waterfront bars," Kara said excitedly as she turned the key in the ignition.

"Sorry, sweetheart, but I'm afraid you're going to have to wait a little longer."

"Why?" she asked, looking over at him curiously as the Jeep idled.

"Because you're not coming with me."

"Adam, that's not fair! I want to help."

He bent his head to give her a quick kiss. "No one ever said life was fair, Kara. Now, if you really want to help, you'll take me back to Colin's house so I can pick up my rental car."

"And what am I supposed to do while you play cops and robbers?"

"You can always finish up my tile," he suggested.

Kara's answer was a brief, pungent curse.

"WELL? Where's your young man?" Maggie Tiernan's bright eyes observed Kara with interest.

"He's on his way to some sleazy waterfront bar for thrills and adventure," she muttered grumpily. "And he's most definitely not my young man."

The elderly woman chuckled. "Try telling that to him," she advised. "And while you're at it, would you care to explain why even the mention of Adam Lassiter makes you blush?"

"This isn't a blush," Kara insisted. "I never blush."

"Of course you don't," Maggie agreed knowingly.

"It's this room; it's like a rain forest in here."

The lavender head bobbed. "It is nice, isn't it?" Maggie's pleased gaze circled the room, enjoying the colorful display of tropical plants.

Recognizing her chance, Kara changed the subject to her grandmother's ingenious green thumb. For the next five minutes they discussed the spectacular crimson blooms of the royal poinciana, the lacy pink and white shower trees, and a new night-blooming cereus Maggie had acquired and had high hopes for.

Unfortunately Kara was soon to discover that her reprieve was only temporary. With the tenacity of a bull terrier worrying a particularly succulent bone, Maggie deftly returned the conversation to its initial topic.

"You and Adam are lovers, aren't you?"

Knowing her grandmother's penchant for speaking her mind, Kara tried not to take offense at the forthright question.

"Really, Grandy," she protested with a weak smile, "that's a very personal question."

Maggie tilted the Belleek shamrock teapot, filling their cups. "It doesn't matter. If you haven't made love yet, you will; there was enough electricity between the two of you to set this entire island on fire."

"Grandy," Kara protested softly as she picked up the silver tongs and dropped a cube of sugar into her tea. Then a second. And a third.

"Disgusting," Maggie muttered as Kara poured a substantial amount of milk into her cup.

"You're the one who taught me to drink tea this way," Kara reminded her grandmother.

"When you were two years old. You're an adult now. Or at least you're supposed to be, although Lord knows you're certainly not acting like one lately."

Kara eyed Maggie over the rim of her cup. Her look of serenity was feigned. "I suppose now you're talking about Adam."

"I always knew you were a bright girl, Kara."

"There's no future for me with Adam Lassiter."

Still-bright eyes, sparkling with intelligence, looked at Kara censoriously. Maggie lifted a snow-white brow. "Are you telling me that you're not going to let things take their natural course because the man hasn't promised you fifty years of married bliss?"

She made it sound so easy, Kara mused. And why not? She had no doubt that if Maggie Tiernan had found herself in Kara's position, she would have reached out for whatever Adam had to offer with both hands. Maggie lived for the moment; in that respect, Kara had thought that she resembled her grandmother as she had gone through the past few years, taking one sun-filled day at a time.

It was coming as a distinct surprise to discover that she was not quite as whimsical as she had thought. Somehow, when no one was looking, the no-nonsense, practical stock of Michael Tiernan's New England ancestors—courtesy of his father, Palmer Winfield—had slipped into the family's gene pool, ultimately ending up in the Tiernans' daughter.

"I'm not like you, Grandy. You had one great passion in your life, which resulted in my father. And when the affair was over and Palmer Winfield dutifully returned to his wife, the automobile heiress, you threw yourself into your work and never looked back. No recriminations, no regrets."

The sudden rattling of the delicate china cup against the saucer captured her attention, and Kara was appalled to realize that her hands were trembling.

Maggie suddenly sat up on the peacock throne chair, her elderly spine as erect as if someone had slipped a rod of cold steel down the back of her lace dress.

"I take back what I said about you being bright, Kara Margaret Tiernan," she shot back, her eyes blazing. "You're a fool if you don't think I had regrets. Recriminations? My God, I loved Palmer—I adored the ground that man walked on. I thought I was going to die when he left me."

For just a fleeting moment, as she observed her grandmother with ill-concealed surprise, Kara was able to see the young woman she once had been: a woman who had obviously experienced many of the same unsettling feelings that Kara herself was currently suffering.

"But you didn't."

"No. As you already pointed out, I had my work. And of course, I had your father."

She reached out and covered Kara's hand with her own beringed one. Blue veins crisscrossed the back of Maggie's hand, but her still-soft skin was the color of gardenias, free of the age spots so many of her contemporaries suffered. As Kara lifted her gaze to Maggie's face, she realized suddenly that her grandmother was still a remarkably beautiful woman.

"Don't let the mistakes of the past stop you from loving, Kara," she said with a sudden, almost desperate urgency. "Adam is different. I know he is. And unlike Palmer, he isn't married."

"Adam is different," Kara agreed quietly. "He's like no one I've ever known, and when I'm with him I feel like a different person."

Comprehension dawned in Maggie's eyes. "You're in love with him."

"No. I don't know. Maybe I am," Kara admitted.

A soft afternoon rain was falling outside the windows of the solarium, and Kara directed her attention toward a scarlet cardinal perched on a twisted branch of a pandanus tree, seeking shelter from the slanting silver drops.

"Would that be so bad?" Maggie asked gently. "What's the worst that can happen?"

"You really want to know?" Kara gave her grandmother a long, challenging look. "What if Adam falls in love with me?"

"I can think of worse fates."

"What if he wants to get married?"

"I'll dance at your wedding," Maggie said without missing a beat.

She didn't understand, Kara thought miserably. None of them did. Adam had been on the island less than a week, and already she had been forced to have this conversation with her mother, her father, and even Colin, when he had telephoned last evening. Not one of them could understand her concern. Was she crazy, Kara wondered. Or were they all blind?

"Can you see me living in San Francisco? Doing whatever it is police chiefs' wives do? I tried living in the pressure cooker of the outside world, and I failed miserably. I couldn't do it again. Not even for Adam."

Maggie didn't argue. "Then Adam will simply have to live here, dear," she assured Kara calmly.

It was the same answer she had gotten from the rest of the family, but the fact that her family agreed to a man—or woman—didn't carry a lot of weight with Kara. She was well aware that all of them, herself included, lived in a fantasyland of their own making. Her grandmother, along with her mother, brother and yes, even her father, had created this world by their artistic efforts; citizenship in the magic realm had been Kara's birthright. But Adam was only a visitor here. When his vacation was over he would be returning to the harsh world of reality. Alone.

"Well," she said briskly as she got up to leave, "we'll never know what Adam would do, will we? Because I'd never in a million years ask him to give up something he's worked his entire life to achieve. So it's a moot point."

She bent down and kissed her grandmother's weathered cheek. "Thanks for the tea, Grandy. It was delicious, as usual."

Maggie beamed. "It wasn't bad, was it? For tea bags."

Kara stared. "Are you telling me—"

"Shh." Maggie put her finger to her lips. "Don't let Larry know that I know about his little subterfuge. He's so proud of his ability to brew excellent tea that I'd hate to disappoint him."

Kara resisted the temptation to laugh. "I promise," she said gravely, struggling to keep a smile from breaking through.

The laughter she had been keeping in escaped as she drove away from her grandmother's house, and for the first time in days, Kara felt absolutely lighthearted. The rain had stopped, and the lingering mist endowed the rising green ramparts with a dawn-of-creation air as a rainbow painted the sky with bold strokes of color.

It was as if the clouds of despair summoned by her indecision concerning Adam had been banished by the brilliant hues of that vibrant sun-kissed arc. Kara vowed that she would grasp this feeling and hold on to it. Whatever the future held, sunshine or rain, she was going to continue to wish on the rainbows.

HE WAS AWARE OF HER the instant she entered the tavern. Every head in the place swiveled in her direction as she stood in the doorway, allowing her eyes to become accustomed to the dim light. When she finally located Adam, she smiled and crossed the room to the bar.

"What the hell are you doing here?" he ground out.

"Having a drink with you. I'll have a mai tai," she said, giving her order to the bartender with a dazzling smile.

"I don't remember giving you permission to come here, Kara," he said under his breath.

"That figures, since I don't recall asking for permission," she said easily, thanking the bartender with yet another warm smile as he placed the drink in front of her.

"That glass probably hasn't been washed in a month," Adam warned as she took a sip of the cool rum drink.

"That's all right," she answered on a gasp, "there's enough alcohol in here to kill any little bacteria that might be foolhardy enough to stick around."

"Speaking of foolhardy—"

Kara placed a placating hand on his arm. "Oh, Adam, please don't be mad at me. I tried to do what you said; I even went up to my grandmother's house. But I couldn't stop thinking of you here. Alone. Possibly in danger."

He shook his head in disgust as he lifted the long-necked beer bottle to his lips. "So you decided to make things dangerous for both of us. Makes sense to me."

"Liz is right," she returned. "You *are* mean. All I wanted to do was to be with you. Do you have any idea how bad I'd feel if you suddenly disappeared like Brett?"

"I'm not going to take off and leave you without saying goodbye, if that's what you're worried about."

"But you are leaving." She could have bitten off her tongue as the incautious words escaped her lips.

Sensing her anxiety, Adam softened his tone. "I have to go back to San Francisco; you knew that from the beginning, Kara."

"For goodness' sake, Adam, there you go again, taking things too seriously." Her desperate gray eyes circled the room, not lighting anywhere. "This is so much fun," she gushed with feigned gaiety. "I feel just like Cagney and Lacey."

Adam was watching her carefully. "Kara—"

She refused to acknowledge the concern in his steady gaze, knowing that to do so would prove her downfall. "Have you found out anything about Brett?"

Aware of the fact that Kara was distressed but not knowing what he could possibly do about it here, now, Adam reluctantly returned his attention to his reason for being in the bar.

"Not a damned thing," he muttered. "It appears the aloha spirit hasn't quite reached the Blue Parrot. At least not when it comes to a mainlander."

"Perhaps I can help." Before Adam could stop her, Kara slid off the stool and made her way to the end of the bar where a group of stevedores were playing a rousing game of electrodart.

"Hey, brah," she said in a silky, sultry voice that made Adam, as he came up behind her, want to wring her neck, "you know where can find da kine scuba man, Brett Britton? Haole here wanna take lessons." She jerked her tawny head in Adam's direction.

"Wasetime to look for him here," the affable young man answered in the relaxed pidgin English Adam had been hearing since entering the bar. "Mo' betta you find his *ipo,* Wainani. . . . Girlfriend," he elaborated for Adam's benefit.

"Liz Forsythe's scuba man's *ipo,*" Kara corrected.

"Scuba man been makin' fastime with Wainani," the man insisted. "Dat lady got mo' dolla than can count. Scuba man buy drinks for the house udda day. He say by'm'by he be rich man."

Kara couldn't believe Brett would leave Liz for another woman. Even one with more money than she could count. "*Mahalo,*" she murmured absently in gratitude as she considered this new aspect of Brett Britton's disappearance.

As the man's black eyes skimmed down Kara's body with unmistakable interest, Adam slipped a folded bill into the pocket of his flowered shirt. "Thanks. Come on, Kara, let's go."

As he checked the denomination of the bill, the stevedore's face lit up in a broad grin. "Hey, brah, *mahalo* yourself."

When two men at a nearby table rose in unison, Adam took Kara's arm. "Kara, it's time to leave."

"But I haven't finished my drink."

"Yes, you have."

"Really, Adam," she complained as she found herself being unceremoniously hurried out of the waterfront tavern, "has anyone ever told you that you can be very high-handed?"

"All the time. And I do my best to live up to it. Now if you can stop arguing, I'd like to get out of here before those Feds come to the mistaken conclusion that we know more about all this than we do."

"Feds?" Kara looked back toward the bar as Adam practically dragged her across the parking lot. "As in FBI?"

"Not the IRS," he agreed grimly. "Although at this point, I wouldn't be surprised to find out that they had a hand in all this, too."

"Had a hand in what?" Kara asked, clearly confused.

Adam opened the door of the rental car. "We'll come back for your Jeep in the morning."

"Fine. I wasn't worried about it," she murmured distractedly. "Adam, what's going on?"

"I don't know," he said as he shoved her ungently into the car. "But I'm sure as hell going to find out."

They drove for a while in silence, immersed in thought. "By the way," Adam growled, "where did you get that dress?"

Kara smoothed the skirt of the snug red sarong. "I borrowed it from a friend who dances in a show at one of the resorts. I didn't have anything that looked appropriate for a place like the Blue Parrot," she added as an afterthought.

"That's a relief."

"What's the matter? Don't you like it?"

"Dammit, Kara, you looked like you were trolling," he complained. "The guy sitting next to me practically fell off his stool when you strolled in the door."

Kara's face lit up with a bright smile. "Why, Adam Lassiter, I do believe you're jealous."

"Don't be silly," he muttered brusquely. "I just don't like you looking like the sort of woman who belongs in that kind of place. Even if it did get us some valuable information."

She leaned over, running her fingers through his hair. "Hey, brah," she murmured silkily into his ear, "you wanna come over to my place, find out da kine woman you got?"

Adam wondered what it was about Kara that made it impossible to remain angry with her. She'd belittled him from the beginning, casting aspersions on his personality, his life-style and his promotion. Despite her insistence that he should relax and enjoy his vacation, she'd gotten him mixed up with a larcenous blonde who was probably going to end up getting him beaten up, shot at or arrested by the federal government. None of which held any vast appeal for him. She'd waltzed into the bar tonight as if she didn't have a care in the world, blatantly and cheerfully defying his orders that she stay home where she belonged. She'd been nothing but a frustrating headache since the moment he'd first seen her, perched atop Colin's damned roof.

She was also the most desirable, intriguing woman he'd ever met. Giving up, as he'd known all along he would, Adam ran his hand up the tantalizing expanse of leg bared by the deep slit in her skirt. "Lady," he growled seductively, "thassa mo betta offer than I get all day."

"IT'S A BOAT," Adam said suddenly as he and Kara ate breakfast in the kitchen of Kara's quaint, weathered-gray home.

From the moment he'd first walked in the door, Adam had decided the house definitely suited her. The blond tone of the bleached oak floor reflected the light of the Hawaiian sun, bathing everything in a warm yellow glow. The furniture was all white wicker and rattan, light and airy, the cushion covers printed with a brilliant array of wild-flowers.

Flowers were everywhere—scarlet and gold hibiscus blossoms floated in a pair of bright blue ceramic bowls, and branches of purple bougainvillea and snowy white olean-der were stuck haphazardly into colored one-of-a-kind bottles. On the sunshine-yellow walls, a veritable garden of oversize tropical flower prints bloomed within the bor-ders of narrow aluminum frames.

The entire atmosphere in the small house—the furni-ture, the flowers, the whimsical figurine made from the leaves of the hala tree—was as lovely and as free-spirited, as simple and unpretentious as its owner. And as different as it was from his high-rise San Francisco apartment, Adam found himself feeling oddly at home.

"What's a boat?" Kara asked as she stirred her coffee.

"*Wainani*. She's not a woman; she's a damned boat."

Kara eyed him curiously over the rim of her cup. "How on earth did you come to that conclusion?"

"It only makes sense," he argued. "Look, the guy's a scuba diver, right?"

She nodded. "Right."

"And he knows these waters pretty damned well."

"Like the back of his hand."

"Let's say, just for argument, that while he's out diving one day, he runs across a sunken wreck."

"One with treasure on it," Kara said, warming to the idea.

"Exactly. So he concocts a plan to get the treasure off the boat without anyone knowing."

"But Liz finds out and turns him in to the FBI?" she asked skeptically. "I'll admit that she appears to be lying about what she knows about all this, but a woman can tell when another woman's in love. And Liz is definitely in love with Brett. She'd never do anything that might get him arrested.

No matter what he'd done." Kara shook her head firmly. "I'm sorry, but that piece just doesn't fit at all, Adam."

"Sure it does." His eyes were gleaming with barely restrained enthusiasm, and as he rubbed his hands together with obvious satisfaction, Kara decided that she loved watching Adam work. His enthusiasm was definitely contagious.

"Let's assume that Britton told Liz about the ship," he continued patiently. "Let's also suppose that the cargo, whatever it is, belongs to the U.S. government."

"All right. So far I'm with you, but..." Kara's voice trailed off as comprehension suddenly dawned. "Liz loves Brett and doesn't want him to go to prison. So without telling him what she's doing, she goes to the FBI to see if she can talk them into paying a reward. A finder's fee. That way—"

"Brett gets more money than he'd make in several lifetimes with that charter business of his, he stays out of jail, he and Liz get married and live happily ever after. That would also explain why she never contacted the police; she's obviously trying to protect him."

That last was certainly news to Kara. Some of the animation faded from her face. "Liz didn't contact the police?"

"Nope. Chief Kanualu didn't know anything about Britton's disappearance or yesterday's vandalism at the shop."

Kara didn't think she'd ever seen Adam look more pleased with himself. Her own expression was openly admiring. "Colin's right, Adam; you are a genius!"

"If I were such a genius, I'd know where Britton is," he exclaimed with ill-concealed frustration. He shook his head. "Come on, sweetheart, we're wasting time. Let's go check the harbor records."

"For sunken ships?"

He ruffled her hair with an easy familiarity. "Now who's a genius?"

10

"WHERE DID I ever get the idea that police work was exciting?" Kara complained on their third day of searching through the stacks of leather-bound journals, seeking some record of the *Wainani*.

"Despite what you've seen on television, most of it is painstaking detail work," Adam said. "Like looking for the proverbial needle in the haystack."

"Well, we couldn't have found a dustier haystack if we'd tried," she complained, wiping at a smudge on her pink T-shirt. "Whatever happened to the computer age?"

"You're the one who pointed out that things are a little slower here on Kauai," he reminded her as he skimmed through yet another thick journal.

"I know," Kara sighed. "But it seems so hopeless, Adam. What if it turns out that the *Wainani* isn't a boat, after all? We will have wasted three valuable days of your vacation."

"It's a boat," he reassured her confidently. "And as for my vacation, I'd never consider any time spent with you wasted."

She managed a weak smile. "Sometimes you can say the nicest things. Thank you. I think I needed that right now."

She sounded tired and uncharacteristically discouraged. Reminding himself that Kara was not used to spending her days in dingy basement storage rooms, searching for the single key that might unlock an entire case, Adam put the heavy book aside and went over to her.

"Did anyone ever tell you that you look terrific with dirt on your cheeks?" he asked as he ran his knuckles over her cheekbone.

"You're just prejudiced."

"Probably so," he agreed easily. "But you still look gorgeous in dirt."

"If you find this appealing, you should see me covered in mud."

A distant flame gleamed in Adam's dark blue eyes. "Now that's an interesting idea. Have you ever considered taking up mud wrestling?"

She arched an auburn brow. "With you?"

He bent his head to kiss her. "Of course. You don't think I'd let you go rolling around in the mud with anyone else, do you?" he asked with an air of possessiveness that should have irritated Kara, but for some strange reason didn't.

"Mud's awfully messy," she murmured as his lips brushed teasingly over hers.

"I know; that's precisely what's supposed to be so much fun about it."

When she tilted her head back to look up at him, the familiar dancing light was back in her eyes. "And exactly who's going to clean up all the muck and mire afterward?"

Adam laughed. "There you go again, revealing that distressing practical streak," he complained good-naturedly. "What am I going to do with you, Kara Tiernan?"

As she placed her hands on his shoulders, her liquid silver gaze spoke volumes. "Funny you should bring that up; I've got a few suggestions along those very same lines."

Feeling the now-familiar stir of desire, Adam kissed her long and lingeringly. "Later."

"Later," she agreed softly.

They had been back at work for less than ten minutes when Kara found it. "Adam!" she called out excitedly. "Here it is! The *Wainani*! She went down in a tropical storm nearly twenty-five years ago on a trip from Oahu to Kauai. You were right."

"Of course," he said easily, leaning down to read over her shoulder. "She's a cargo barge. Let's see what's on the manifest."

"Just the usual," she murmured, reading through the lengthy list. "Food, hardware, cars—" As she turned the page, Kara drew in a sharp breath. "And the sugar cooperative's monthly payroll!"

"Two hundred and fifty thousand dollars in cash?" Adam asked incredulously.

"It wasn't all that unusual," she explained. "The workers didn't really trust banks. Most of them preferred to get their pay in cash."

"No wonder Britton was excited," Adam mused. "A quarter of a million tax-free dollars would be a nice little nest egg for anyone to start a marriage with." He frowned as he continued to read the record. "This is interesting."

"What?"

"The Coast Guard received a distress signal right before the *Wainani* went down."

"What's so unusual about that?" Kara questioned. "They probably receive a lot of SOSs during storms."

"Probably do," he agreed. "But how many of those ships do you think say that they're being boarded by pirates?"

Every vestige of fatigue vanished as Kara's eyes filled with excitement. "Pirates?"

Adam nodded. His mouth was a grim, taut line. "Pirates. I think it's time we had another little talk with Liz."

"This is getting more thrilling by the minute," Kara said as they returned up the coast. "Imagine the *Wainani* being boarded by pirates only minutes before it went down with all that cash on board!"

"Now all we have to do is find out who hired the pirates," Adam said.

She glanced over at him. "And you can do that, can't you, Adam?"

He grinned as he patted her thigh. "Piece of cake."

She was as elated as he'd ever seen her, and to tell the truth, he wasn't feeling so bad himself. After being cooped up behind a desk for so many years, he'd forgotten the thrill of the chase. Only two things dampened his enthusiasm, the first was the fact that they still didn't have a clue as to Britton's whereabouts, and the second was the nondescript beige sedan that had been following them all day. A quick glance in the rearview mirror confirmed that it was still there.

"PIRATES?" Liz stared at Adam as if he had suddenly grown another head. "The *Wainani* went down with pirates on board?"

"Then you do know what Brett's been up to," Adam said mildly.

"Only some of it," she insisted. "I knew he'd found the *Wainani*; I knew he intended to salvage it. But I didn't know anything about pirates. And I certainly don't know where he is! Pirates?" The last was said with a wail that Kara knew was not feigned. Liz's hands shook violently as she tried to light a cigarette.

"Here," Adam said, taking the lighter from her hand, "let me."

Liz gave him an appreciative look as she inhaled deeply. "I was afraid you'd find out about the *Wainani*," she said in a flat voice. "Especially after Kara told me all about your being up for chief of police. But I was getting desperate; you were my only hope."

"But I thought you wanted Adam to find Brett," Kara objected.

"I did. I just didn't want him to find out about the *Wainani* at the same time."

Kara was clearly confused. "Why? Surely you don't think Adam would steal the money?"

"Of course not." Liz was on her feet, pacing nervously back and forth across the floor of the candy shop. She'd closed the shop immediately on their arrival. One look at Adam's grim face had been all she needed to know that they were about to have a long-overdue conversation. "But I was afraid if he knew what Brett intended to do, he'd arrest him."

"My jurisdiction doesn't cover Kauai," he pointed out.

She shot him a narrow glance. "All you'd have to do is tell Chief Kanualu what you know, and Brett would be spending our honeymoon in jail."

"But Adam wouldn't do that," Kara said quickly. "Would you, Adam?"

"I'm a lot more interested in keeping your fiancé alive than in putting him behind bars," he confirmed. "Speaking of which, what exactly did you tell the Feds?"

"I didn't think you'd bought that story about the affair," Liz admitted. "I knew that it wasn't very convincing, but I didn't have time to concoct a story. How was I to know you'd find out I'd been to their offices?"

"I told you he was brilliant," Kara put in.

"So you did," Liz agreed dryly. "As for the FBI, I didn't tell them anything; all I did was give them a hypothetical case and ask if the government routinely gave rewards for the recovery of stolen goods."

"And you thought they'd buy that?" Adam asked incredulously.

Liz nodded. "They certainly seemed to. In fact, to tell you the truth, they didn't appear at all interested in anything I had to say."

Adam knew better, but he didn't see any point in muddying the waters at this point. Since Liz had actually been cooperating for once, he didn't want to take a chance on her clamming up.

"Where is the *Wainani*, Liz?" he asked quietly.

"I don't know. Brett said it would be safer all around if he was the only one who knew where she went down," she added, seeing Adam's disbelieving look.

"Do you know if he had a map showing the spot?"

Liz shook her head dejectedly. "I don't think so. That's what the people who trashed our shops were looking for, wasn't it? The map."

"It would appear so," Adam agreed.

"I was so worried about the authorities finding out what Brett was doing. But the men who tore the place apart weren't FBI men, were they?"

Adam's lips were a taut, grim line. "No."

Her blond hair was like a curtain, hiding her face as she bent her head. When she finally lifted her gaze, her tragic green eyes observed Adam bleakly. "Brett's in a great deal of danger, isn't he, Adam?"

Adam knew the gallant thing to do would be to lie, to assure Kara's friend that she'd have her missing fiancé back in time for dinner. "I think he is, Liz," he said gravely instead.

She digested that for a long, thoughtful moment. "Then you'll just have to find him before something terrible happens to him, won't you?"

"Of course he will," Kara insisted bracingly. "Won't you, Adam?"

"Since I've always been a sucker for beautiful damsels in distress," Adam said philosophically, "I suppose I don't have any choice."

"Liz is beautiful, isn't she, Adam?" Kara asked as they drove away from Kauai Kandy.

Knowing he was in a no-win situation, Adam merely shrugged. "I suppose so; if you go for that type."

She slanted him a sideways glance. "Don't all men prefer blondes?"

"Not necessarily. Are you by any chance fishing for compliments?"

The blush that was the bane of every redhead's life rose brilliantly in her cheeks. Folding her arms, Kara directed her gaze steadfastly out the window. "Of course not; don't be silly."

He reached over and took her hand. "If it's any comfort, Kara, the beautiful damsel in distress I was referring to was you."

A smile lit her gray eyes. "Thank you, Adam," she said softly. "That's a very nice thing to say."

"It's the truth," he said simply as he glanced up at the rearview mirror, not at all surprised to see the beige sedan following at a discreet distance.

The car stayed with them, parking nearby when they stopped for a showing of Michael Tiernan's paintings at the Kahn Gallery in the Coconut Plantation Market Place. Adam had been to several gallery shows over the years, but none as unique as this one.

The white walls were covered with abstract paintings, which were as colorful as they were horrendous. Watching Michael circulate through the crowd, drinking in the enthusiastic compliments, Adam decided that he had never seen a happier man. To no one's surprise, it appeared that the show would sell out before everyone was to attend a celebratory luau at the Tiernan home.

"Would you be very angry at me if I showed up a little late to the luau?" Adam asked, taking Kara aside. "I need to slip away for a short while."

"Of course not. I can always get a ride with Maggie and Ling Su. Where are you going?"

"I want to try to get a line on those pirates."

"Tonight? Won't the trail be awfully cold?" Kara privately prided herself on knowing a bit of investigative jargon. All those years of faithfully watching *Magnum P.I.* every week were beginning to pay off.

"I think Britton's probably heated it up," Adam replied.

"Adam, people know you're looking for Brett; you could be in danger, too."

"Don't worry about me; I know what I'm doing."

"And what exactly are you doing?"

"Going back to the Blue Parrot," he informed her reluctantly. It was bad enough that Kara had walked into that dive in the middle of the afternoon. He damned well didn't want her showing up there at night.

Despite his reassuring words, Kara was overcome with a growing sense of anxiety. "Not alone, you're not."

"I'm not taking you with me, Kara. Not this time."

"But—"

"No."

Kara had spent enough time with Adam to know when arguing, even the most feminine wheedling, would be fruitless. She put her hand on his arm. "Promise me you'll be careful," she whispered.

Despite the dangerous turn this case had taken, Adam found himself unreasonably pleased by Kara's obvious show of concern. It was nice to have someone worry about you, he decided.

"I wouldn't know how to be anything but." He kissed her. "See you at the luau."

Kara seemed about to say something else, but instead merely nodded. Worry lingered in her gray eyes as she watched him leave the gallery. Despite his reassuring words, she could not forget that night so many years ago when he had crept through a dark and dangerous warehouse. Alone.

THE NIGHT WAS ALIVE WITH FIRE. Music. Perfume. If Adam had found Kauai to be a different world than the one he toiled in back on the mainland, tonight he felt as if he'd stepped into a time machine and been shot backward at least a hundred years.

Flaming torches glowed a brilliant orange against the star-studded black sky; the throb of Hawaiian drums echoed the pounding of waves against the dark lava ramparts. The sultry night air was perfumed by myriad flowers adorning the huge backyard, their hues rivaled by the brilliant aloha shirts and muumuus worn by the guests. At the sight of all those colorfully flowered adaptations of the voluminous Mother Hubbards the missionaries had forced on the Hawaiians, Adam wondered who had converted whom.

He spotted Kara across the yard, laughing with the broad-faced bartender, and decided he had never seen anything as lovely as she looked that night. She was wearing a slim version of a Chinese tunic, slit on the side to reveal an enticing glimpse of golden thigh. The blaze of colors would have put a bird of paradise to shame. As if aware of his silent scrutiny, she turned, a faint blush drifting into her cheeks.

"Thank God you're back," Kara said breathlessly as she threw herself into his arms and kissed him heatedly, desperately. "Do you have any idea how worried I've been about you?"

"I told you I could handle things," Adam reminded her.

"I know. But I was still going crazy." She ran her hands over him, as if searching for hidden injuries. "Are you sure you're all right?"

"Positive. Although if you want, we can go somewhere a little more private and you can check me over for broken bones."

Her eyes were bright with a tantalizing blend of relief and desire. "Remind me of that offer when we get home."

"You've got a deal."

"Did you learn anything that will put us closer to Brett?"

"Nothing."

"Oh, dear. And we were getting so close."

On the drive up the coast from the Blue Parrot, Adam had decided not to tell Kara that he had a line on the man who had employed the unlucky pirates. When the time came to confront the man, Adam didn't want her anywhere in the vicinity.

"Don't worry, something'll turn up. It always does. Here—I brought you something," he said with an encouraging smile as he bent to pick up the gift he'd dropped when she had thrown herself into his arms.

"Oh, Adam," Kara whispered, as he put the lei over her head, "what a lovely surprise."

"The woman at the shop told me that the ancient Hawaiian chiefs used these flowers to make leis for Pele, so I figured they'd be perfect for you."

Her fingers plucked the feathery scarlet ohia lehua blossoms. "They used to be considered sacred," she said softly. "Thank you."

He shrugged. "I like buying you things, Kara."

His words were simple, but the sudden solemnity of his tone threatened to be her undoing. "Speaking of buying things," she said, hurriedly changing the subject, "did I happen to mention that what you did this afternoon was one of the nicest things I've ever seen you do?"

"Buying three of your father's paintings?" Adam asked with a shrug as he pulled her down to sit beside him on the lawn. "That wasn't being nice; I liked them."

She glanced down at the glass of Scotch in his hand. "How many of those things did you have at the Blue Parrot? Those paintings were the worst of the bunch."

Adam chuckled as he reached over and cupped her chin in his long fingers. "They couldn't have been," he said lightly, giving her a quick kiss. "They were all of you."

"How on earth could you tell?"

"Simple. I looked at them, felt the heat and knew it couldn't be anyone else." He tilted his head back and grinned down at her. "Have I told you that you look absolutely *nani* this evening?"

It had not escaped Kara's notice that little by little native words had begun slipping into Adam's vocabulary. That grim business-suited man she had first seen struggling along the beach had undergone an amazing metamorphosis into the Adam Lassiter who was now sprawled lazily beside her on the lawn. He was gradually succumbing to the philosophy of *hoomanawanui*—let's take it easy—with an ease that almost had Kara believing he could be happy here in paradise. With her.

"*Mahalo,*" she answered softly.

Her gray eyes took a leisurely tour of the superb male body only inches away. Adam was clad in a white knit polo shirt depicting a trio of surfers—she still hadn't managed to talk him into a flowered aloha shirt—which displayed to advantage the lithe muscles of his upper arms and firm torso. His khaki shorts revealed long bronze legs that would make any woman's heart flutter. The expensive Italian loafers had given way to a pair of practical beach sandals.

All in all, Kara thought that Adam had never looked better.

"You don't look so bad yourself," she said. "For a *malihini*."

His fingers skimmed over her face before tangling in her wind-ruffled hair. "Ah, but you're prejudiced."

She linked her hands around the back of his neck. "You bet I am." Without another word, their mouths met in mutual pleasure. As Kara's lips clung to his, the out-of-control pounding of her blood seemed to be synchronized with the primitive beat of the drums.

The soft scent of flowers enveloped Adam's head like a fragrant cloud, threatening to drive him mad. He swore softly against Kara's lips as the deep, foghorn sound of conch shells being blown encouraged an answering roar from the crowd.

"They've just taken the pig from the *imu*," Kara explained, pointing toward the subterranean oven.

She linked her fingers with his, leading him from the shadows into the circle of light created by the flaming torches. Adam soon found himself seated between Kara and Michael, facing an extraordinary array of exotic dishes.

"I like this," Adam offered, tentatively taking a taste of the *opihi*, a salty black mollusk that reminded him of a small clam.

"Try this *lomi lomi* salmon," Kara suggested, holding out a piece of the pink-fleshed fish.

"You've just caught my interest, sweetheart," Adam growled. Only the night before she'd treated him to an incredibly sensual massage—or *lomi lomi*—with warmed coconut oil. Of course he'd reciprocated. One thing had led to another and soon they were making love.

Kara laughed. "The salmon's massaged with a marinade of chopped onions and tomatoes before cooking."

Adam's lips closed around her fingers. "Good," he decided. "But I think I prefer *lomi lomi Kara*."

The sensuality swirling in his dark eyes thrilled her. "You haven't tried the *poi*," she murmured, trying to maintain her equilibrium. It was always this way. He could make her want him with a mere look, a single touch.

"I'll try it later," he said, toying with the natural pearl adorning her earlobe. His light touch kindled a now-familiar heat.

The need for him crept into her, dark and insistent. "You haven't experienced a real luau without tasting *poi*," she whispered weakly.

Without taking his eyes from hers, Adam dipped two fingers into the wooden bowl of purplish-brown starch made from pounded taro root. It tasted like library paste.

"Terrific," he said. "Can we go home now?"

Michael, who had been arguing with Maggie over whether the chicken luau was better with taro or spinach leaves, overheard Adam's request.

"Oh, you can't leave yet," he insisted. "The dancing's just beginning."

Adam sighed as he ran his knuckles down the side of Kara's face, trailing his fingers along her firm, uplifted jaw. "Later."

She felt as if she were melting. "Later," she agreed in a whisper.

"The hula began as a religious dance," Kara remarked in her best tour-guide fashion. "It reflected the deep cosmic piety of the Hawaiians, their love and awe of the tremendous forces of nature that surrounded them. The first hula in history was danced by Pele's favorite sister, Laka, in order to amuse the fire goddess."

"And thus keep her from losing her temper with disastrous results," Adam guessed, watching the beautiful dance being performed by a troop of attractive young men and women.

The percussive rhythms that accompanied the dancers came from wooden sticks struck together, producing sounds like those of a xylophone. Other musicians clicked together small stones like castanets, or shook seed-filled gourds to the pulsating beat, reminding Adam of Latin American maracas.

"You're supposed to watch their hands," Kara explained. "They tell the story."

Adam's attention was momentarily captured by a lissome young thing whose undulating hips were tracing a perfect figure eight. "You watch the hula your way and I'll watch it mine," he suggested with a wicked grin.

Kara laughed. "It's just a good thing I'm not a jealous woman, Adam Lassiter, or you'd end up with this bowl over your head and *poi* dripping off your chin."

"Good thing," he murmured after a long pause, wondering why that idea no longer pleased him.

Before he could dwell any longer on the thought, Kara was dragged from her seat on the lawn by a loincloth-clad male dancer, to the delight of the guests. She laughed as she threw back her head and began to dance along with the others.

"I think I owe you an apology," Michael surprised Adam by saying suddenly.

"An apology?" he asked distractedly, his attention riveted on Kara.

The movements of her slender hands and the graceful steps of her bare feet appeared to beckon to some unseen lover as the undeniably sensual sway of her hips pulled the floral silk against her thighs in a way that made Adam bite back a groan. When the male dancer put his broad dark hands on those slowly circling hips, Adam felt a fire begin to burn in his gut.

"About you and Kara," Michael explained. "Her mother and I can't remember seeing her happier."

"She's made me happy, too," Adam said.

Or at least he had been happy, until that half-naked guy started touching Kara that way. Her hips moved in a hypnotic rhythm with the pounding beat of the drums. A strident, demanding sound infiltrated his consciousness, but still Adam could not drag his gaze from Kara.

"I'm afraid I'm going to have to leave for a while," Kara's father said as he turned off the small black beeper attached to his belt. "Debbie Akana's baby was due last week; I'll bet my new easel little Maximino's about to make an appearance."

It took a concentrated effort, but Adam managed to turn his attention toward the older man. "It must keep you busy, maintaining a general practice."

"It's an around-the-clock job," Michael agreed cheerfully. "But I love it."

"Do you ever regret not specializing?" Adam asked, genuinely curious. Although family practice had made a comeback of sorts in the past few years, general practitioners were still a minority.

"I did specialize," Kara's father corrected Adam amiably.

"On Kauai?"

Michael laughed at that, deep bass drumrolls that had Adam feeling inexplicably foolish for even bringing the subject up. "New York," he corrected. "I was chief of surgery at Mount Sinai."

Adam knew he was staring but couldn't help himself. "How could you leave a prestigious position like that to deliver babies on some remote island?"

Michael's smiling face suddenly turned infinitely serious. "At the time, I wasn't sure that I could," he admitted. "But then one day Althea asked me if I was happy."

His expression softened, and Adam had the feeling that Michael Tiernan was back in New York City. "Damnedest question she'd ever asked," he murmured, as if to himself.

"Were you?"

"To tell you the truth, I'd never stopped to consider whether I really liked what I was doing. From the time I entered college, I just kept doing what was expected of me. Medical school, internship, residency...

"It took Althea to make me aware that I'd turned into an automaton. Turn the key in the morning and I'd go to the hospital, where each day I became more of a mechanic than a doctor. I never really knew my patients; I only knew their hearts or their gall bladders or their kidneys."

He grinned. "So we packed up Althea's chisels and my black bag and moved back to my childhood home, where I began seeing patients as people again. Now I know enough to make sure that there's a night-light in the room when little Keoke Santos has his tonsils out because he's been afraid of the dark since he got lost in that lava cave last year.

"I also know that I'd better pick up some lemon drops for Debbie before I go to the hospital because her husband, who usually supplies her with a bag a day, has been stuck on the Big Island all week at National Guard camp.

"Regret not specializing?" he asked, turning serious again. "I am specializing, Adam. In people." He flashed another grin that reminded Adam suddenly of Kara. Then he was gone.

Adam would have liked to ponder Michael Tiernan's unexpected story for a while, but Kara chose that moment to suddenly appear in front of him.

"Want to dance?" she asked, holding out her arms and giving him the most dazzling smile he'd ever seen.

Adam glanced around, realizing that while he'd been engrossed in his brief conversation with Michael, the majority of guests had been engaged in varyingly successful interpretations of the hula.

"I think I'll leave the dancing to you." He got up from the lawn to stand next to her. "By the way, you were definitely off the mark when you said you didn't have any talents, sweetheart. I can't remember when I've seen anything as sexy as you doing the hula."

His eyes flamed as they took a slow, leisurely tour of her body, clad so enticingly in the brilliant silk dress. "Did I tell you how gorgeous you look in this thing?" he asked, skimming his palms down her sides.

Kara lifted her hands to his shoulders. "You certainly did. And if you like this, Adam, wait until you see what's underneath it." Her voice was low, husky and unmistakably inviting.

As the elemental beat of the drums quickened, fire surged through Adam's veins. It was all he could do not to make love to Kara right then and there, in full sight of her family and friends.

"Ready to go home yet?" he asked hopefully.

"Captain, I thought you'd never ask," she said with a merry silver laugh.

THE PHONE CALL came shortly after 2:00 a.m. Kara dragged her hands through her sleep-tangled hair as she listened to Adam's end of the conversation. His short, cryptic statements told her nothing.

"Who was that?" she asked after he'd hung up.

He got out of bed and pulled on a pair of slacks. "Nobody important; go back to sleep."

"If it wasn't anyone important, why are you getting dressed? And what are you doing with that?" Her eyes widened as he pulled a revolver out of the dresser drawer and stuck it in the back of his belt.

"I've got to go out for a while."

"Where?"

"Just out. I'll be back before you know it."

The gun was the deciding factor for Kara. "I'm coming with you," she said, throwing back the sheet.

"The hell you are."

"Adam, you only got involved in this entire mess because I talked you into helping my best friend; think how I'd feel if you were hurt."

"Think how I'd feel if *you* were hurt," he responded gruffly. The very idea sent ice water into his veins. He grabbed her arms. "Don't you understand—I care about you, Kara. Probably too damned much."

His intense expression made her stomach flutter. "I care about you, too, Adam. And I promise not to get in your way. But please let me come with you."

As he looked down into her earnest face, Adam felt as if he were drowning in deep pools of molten silver. "Dammit, this is crazy."

"Please?" she wheedled prettily.

He dragged his hand wearily over his face. What had ever made him think he could keep Kara from doing whatever she wanted to do? Adam was well acquainted with Tiernan stubbornness, since Kara's brother had always had more than his share of that quality. But though Adam had always admired Colin's tenacity, he was finding Kara's damned willfulness unreasonably frustrating.

"When we get out to the island, you're staying on the plane," he warned sternly.

Sensing his acquiescence, Kara began to throw on her clothes. "What island?" she asked as she pulled a yellow T-shirt over her head.

"The one where they're holding Britton. Do we have a deal or don't we?"

"Whatever you say, Adam," she returned sweetly. "Brett's been on one of the islands this entire time?"

"He's only been there since this morning. When he sobered up and realized he'd mouthed off in the bar, he did a vanishing act in the hope of putting everyone off his trail. It took the goons working for the syndicate who had hired the hit on the *Wainani* this long to find him. From what I could find out, they're holding him until their boss arrives here tonight from the mainland."

"If they're holding him captive, then they don't know where the *Wainani* is," Kara said thoughtfully.

"Probably not. It's obvious that they ransacked the shop looking for a map; Britton must have done something right for a change and hidden it someplace none of us have thought of."

"It appears so. What island is he on?"

"Tern," he answered, naming one of the northwestern, or leeward, islands.

"Tern Island? But that's a wildlife refuge."

"Then these guys should feel right at home," he countered. "Are you ready?"

"Almost. Won't it be difficult to hire a plane and pilot at this hour?" she asked.

"We won't have to, because I've had one waiting at the airport for the past eight hours."

"What a lucky coincidence," she murmured. "That you'd hire a plane this very evening. Even after your visit to the Blue Parrot didn't turn up anything new."

"I found out Britton was on one of the uninhabited islands," Adam admitted. "But I didn't know until that phone call exactly which one."

"You lied to me at the luau, didn't you, Adam?" she asked calmly.

"I thought it was best."

"Don't you think that was rather presumptuous of you?"

The movement of his jaw suggested that Adam was grinding his teeth. "If it's presumptuous to want to keep you alive, then I guess I was being presumptuous." He glanced pointedly at his watch. "We're wasting time here, Kara."

She gave him an acquiescent smile as she zipped up her khaki shorts. "I'm ready whenever you are, Adam."

His only response was a muffled oath, but as they walked out to the Jeep, Kara thought she detected a ghost of a smile on his tight lips.

11

WHEN THEY REACHED the airport at Lihue, Adam led her directly to a Piper Apache parked at the end of the runway. When the pilot saw Kara, he looked disapproving.

"Don't tell me she's coming along," he said in a tone that showed exactly how little he thought of the idea.

"She'll be okay," Adam assured him. "She's promised to stay on the plane."

The pilot, a grim-faced individual in his early fifties with an iron-gray crew cut, shrugged. "It's your funeral," he muttered as he turned his attention to preflight details.

"Nice crew you've hired," Kara said to Adam as they boarded the twin-engine plane. "If the pilot's any example of the hospitality on this airline, I can't wait to meet the flight attendants."

"It's a no-frills flight," Adam said amiably, ignoring her acid tone. "We're going to have to serve ourselves."

Kara paused as she buckled her seat belt. "Don't mind if I do," she murmured, leaning over to give him a kiss. "Whatever can I do to thank you for including me in this adventure?"

His fingers cradled the back of her head as Adam held the kiss for a deliriously long time. "I'll accept that as a down payment," he said, brushing his thumb against her smiling lips. "We'll discuss how you can pay off the rest of the debt once we get back home."

Kara wondered briefly if Adam had noticed his slip of the tongue in calling Colin's house home. Deciding that this was no time to bring up what was a perilously personal question, she nodded. "Whatever you think is fair," she agreed, lowering her voice as the pilot climbed into the cockpit of the small four-seater plane. Within minutes they were airborne.

"You know, of course, that your girlfriend's marrying herself an idiot," Adam said as they raced through the night. Outside the windows the sky was filled with brilliant, twinkling stars, and down below the silver moon-gilded water seemed to go on forever.

"I'll admit Brett never seemed overly brilliant," Kara agreed. "But don't you think you're being a bit hard on him?"

"Not nearly as hard as that syndicate boss is going to be if we don't get to him first."

"You said he was coming from the mainland?"

"L.A.," Adam agreed. "Stevenson's a sharp operator. We've been trying to get something concrete on the guy for months. I sure as hell never expected to nail him down here." He shook his head. "Funny thing was, the guy had written the barge off as lost years ago."

"Until Brett got drunk and told everyone in the Blue Parrot that the *Wainani* was going to make him wealthy," Kara guessed.

"Got it on the first try," he said, amused at the way Kara was practically trembling with excitement. She reminded him of a Thoroughbred at the starting gate. But she wasn't alone. The idea of a nighttime rescue raid had his own adrenaline running high. Adam reminded himself to remain cool. Calm. For Kara's sake.

She looked up at him with sober admiration. "You are the smartest man I've ever met, Adam. No wonder they're going to make you police chief."

He wrapped his arms around her. Right then he didn't want to think about his job; he didn't even want to think about Britton, the crime boss or the pirated payroll. He only wanted to feel how perfectly Kara Tiernan fitted into his arms.

"Look at those stars," he murmured. "You never see stars like that in the city. Too many lights."

"And smog," she whispered, resting her head on his shoulder and trying to relax. "How much longer?"

"Not long. There's an old navy landing field dating from World War II on the island; these days it's used to deliver supplies to a small group of Coast Guardsmen stationed on the island to broadcast signals to ships and planes to help them plot their positions.

"As soon as we land, I'll go in and get Britton. The whole thing should be over in ten, fifteen minutes." He smiled at her. "Then you can start thinking about ways to pay off your debt."

"Adam," she began hesitantly, "about my staying on the plane—"

"No." He gripped her chin, fixing her with an almost angry look. "No arguments, Kara. We made a deal and I have every intention of holding you to it."

She reached up, rubbing at the deep lines that bracketed his mouth. "Has anyone ever told you that you look very sexy when you're laying down the law?"

"Dammit, Kara—"

"Really, Adam, that rough, macho behavior is very exciting. Even if it is outrageously chauvinistic," she added somewhat sadly. "Perhaps if we discuss this reasonably, we can find a middle ground."

"After this is over, we can discuss it all you want. For the rest of the night, I'm the boss."

Kara recognized the tone instantly. Further arguing was going to get her nowhere. "Of course, Adam," Kara answered with an assumed tranquillity but an inward tremor. "Whatever you say."

He was looking at her suspiciously when the pilot called out that they'd reached their destination. A moment later they were landing on the runway. At the sudden intrusion of the plane, a blizzard of terns took to the sky. Kara's heart was pounding and she couldn't remember any time when she had felt more alive.

Adam didn't trust Kara's atypical acquiescence, but short of tying her up, he didn't know what to do except give her one last warning. "Remember, whatever happens, you are not to leave this plane," he ordered gruffly.

She dipped her bright head. "I remember." Adam didn't believe a word of her softly issued promise.

With his flashlight cutting through the dark like a laser, he easily located the shack at the northernmost end of the island. It was precisely where his informant had told him it would be. From what he could tell from his vantage point in the bushes, there were no guards posted outside. He smiled grimly. So far, so good.

Making a motion with his arm, he instructed the pilot, who had accompanied him, to go around the back of the house and wait for his prearranged signal. Without a word the man drifted into the shadows.

Adam glanced down at the illuminated dial of his watch. There was still time before he would make his move. He was just congratulating himself when out of the corner of his eye he caught a flash of yellow fabric. A moment later Kara slipped up beside him.

"Dammit, woman," he snapped furiously, "whatever happened to keeping a promise?"

"I had my fingers crossed. Is Brett in there?"

"Yes. Now get back to the damned plane."

"I'm not leaving you," she whispered firmly. "I'm sorry, Adam, but I've given this a great deal of thought and have come to the conclusion that I couldn't bear not knowing what was happening to you."

Another quick glance at his watch showed that he was out of time. Swearing softly, he reached for the gun in the back of his belt. "Since I don't have time to argue with you, you can stay." He pressed his fingers against her lips. "Not another word. And so help me if you move from this spot, I'll beat you black and blue."

"You'd never hit me," she said with calm assurance.

Adam didn't argue the point. There was no need. "Just stay put."

Her eyes gleaming with excitement, Kara nodded. A moment later he moved away, signaling her once again to remain where she was. Then he disappeared into the thick tropical foliage. The only sounds were the lonely rustle of the night wind, the soft sigh of the surf and Kara's heart as it pounded in her ears.

When the explosive sound of a gunshot shattered the night, Kara instinctively crouched down and wrapped her arms around herself. Another shot rang out, fading into the darkness as the night fell silent once again. The ominous quiet was unnerving.

With the gunshots still ringing in her ears, Kara made her way stealthily toward the shack, following Adam's example by keeping hidden in the shadows as best she could. She hadn't realized she had been holding her breath until she looked through the open door and saw Adam standing in the center of the room, his gun pointed at a pair of grim musclebound men Kara assumed to be Brett's captors. Standing next to Adam was the pilot, his own gun drawn. His casual ease with the dangerous situation told Kara that piloting charter planes was probably not his usual occupation.

Nearby sat Brett, bound hand and foot to a wooden chair, a filthy gag over his mouth. His handsome face bore the ugly black-and-blue marks of an earlier struggle, and as he stared at the scene unfolding before him, his blue eyes were wide with fear.

If he was at all surprised to see Kara run through the open door, Adam didn't show it. "Since you're here, why don't you make yourself useful and release Britton, Kara?" he asked calmly. "While Mathison and I take care of these two."

She stared mutely at the two men backed against the wall. One had a stained handkerchief wrapped around his hand. It was blood, Kara realized. He'd been shot. As Adam could so easily have been. A rushing sound filled her head, and her knees went suddenly weak.

When her face turned dangerously pale, Adam reached out and took hold of her shoulder. "Kara? Are you all right?" His voice was as gentle as she'd ever heard it.

Kara shook her head to clear it. "Fine," she assured him faintly. "I'm fine."

"Take a deep breath."

Kara did as he'd instructed, relieved when the fresh air cleared the cobwebs from her mind. She tossed her head as she accepted the knife Adam was holding out to her. "Really, Adam, I'm quite all right; you're behaving as if I've never seen a criminal before."

He had just opened his mouth to comment when a trio of men burst through the open door, guns drawn, faces grim. When Kara looked as if she was going to faint for the second time in as many minutes, Adam quickly put his arm around her.

"You guys missed all the fun," he drawled.

"We thought we'd leave that to you," Chief Kanualu answered, a broad grin splitting his dark face. "Professional courtesy, and all that."

"I appreciate it," Adam said. "How'd we do with Stevenson?"

"The federal boys took him into custody as soon as his plane touched down." The police chief shook his head. "Unfortunately he didn't seem to appreciate our aloha spirit."

"I can't understand that," Adam said with a smile of his own.

"Neither can I," Manny Kanualu agreed. "After all, it's not as if we greet every *haole* who arrives in the islands personally."

He beamed with obvious satisfaction as he tipped his hat toward Kara. "Aloha, Kara. Nice to see you again."

"YOU HAD THE POLICE in on this from the beginning," she accused Adam much later. They were lying in his bed, arms wrapped around each other.

Adam brushed a strand of fiery hair away from her face. "Not exactly from the beginning, but once I figured out what was going down, I thought the least I could do was share the information. I know I hate it when some other jurisdiction is messing around in my precinct without informing me ahead of time. It's also a good way to get shot.

"Besides, once those FBI guys started following us, I didn't have any choice but to fill them in before they got the wrong idea and decided we were working with Britton."

"The FBI was following us?"

He nodded.

"I never saw them."

His lips trailed around her ear. "That was the idea. If you'd noticed them, they weren't doing their job."

She shivered delightedly as his teeth lightly tugged her earlobe. "You saw them," she managed to gasp.

"I'm a pro, remember?"

How could she forget that, with the thought of his leaving to pick up the reins of his career hanging over their heads? "That was nice the way you told everyone that Brett had every intention of turning the money over to the FBI."

Adam shrugged as he ran his hand down her side. The lure of her satiny skin was more than he could resist. "Maybe he really did have that in mind all along. You didn't see him arguing, did you?"

His mouth forced a sizzling path along the slope of Kara's breasts, and her voice grew husky with desire as she tried to concentrate on their conversation. "Would you have argued if you'd been in his shoes?"

"Hell, no." The damp heat of his mouth moved with tantalizing slowness down her body, leaving trails of exquisite lightning.

"You lied to me, Adam. Twice."

"And you lied to me." Sighing heavily, he reluctantly stopped his seductive kisses and lifted himself up on his forearms. "Dammit, Kara, do you have any idea how much danger you could have been in?"

She smiled up at him, framing his scowling face with her palms. "Don't be silly, Adam. I was with you."

He tried to remain angry, but his eyes brimmed with amusement. "I think it's a toss-up," he said finally.

She pressed her lips against his. "What?"

"Which one of us is going to drive the other crazier."

Kara could feel his smile against her mouth. "You're probably right," she agreed cheerfully. "But think how much fun we'll have in the meantime."

With a groan that was part agreement, part anticipation, Adam lowered his body onto hers, locking her securely under him with his thigh. That was the last either of them had to say for a very long time.

THIS WAS, Kara considered happily, as she awoke the next morning, a delicious way to live. She leaned over and pressed a quick kiss against Adam's tanned cheek before getting up. As she slid out from under the sheets, taking care not to wake him, her eyes drifted to the wall beside the bed.

Beside her father's paintings of her, on a piece of yellow legal paper tacked to the wall, were listed the phone numbers of the governor, the mayor, the police commissioner, several city councilmen and every police captain in San Francisco. Kara felt an unreasonable hatred for the list; every time she looked at it, she was reminded that Adam's work was—and would always be—his life. As well as his first love.

Refusing to dwell on the negative, Kara left the house to take her customary morning walk along the beach. The sharp tang of the salt air cleared her head, and the comforting swish of the warm tropical water against her ankles soothed the anxiety created by thoughts of Adam's inevitable return to California. Fully restored to her usual good humor, she skipped up the steps and entered the house. Her smile faded when she discovered Adam on the telephone. His dark frown left her no doubt that the call was business, not pleasure.

"It's the commissioner," he scrawled on a notepad beside the phone.

Kara's heart skipped a beat. Although it certainly hadn't been the first time he had interrupted their peaceful interlude, the frown lines etched on Adam's brow, gave Kara the distinct feeling that this telephone call was different from the others. This was the one that was going to take Adam away from her.

"I've got work to do; I'll see you later," she said.

Adam caught her by the wrist. "Wait a minute," he said before turning his attention back to his caller. "Jack, give me just a minute, okay? Something's come up."

He covered the receiver with his free hand and frowned as his gaze swept her face. "I thought, now that we've gotten your friend's fiancé back safe and sound, that we were going to Fern Grotto this morning."

"We were," she agreed. "But that was before the commissioner called." She could not keep resentment from hardening her tone.

"Forget the commissioner," he said quietly. "He doesn't have anything to do with us."

Doesn't he? Kara was tempted to ask. Don't they all? But that would be breaking the rules she had insisted on from the beginning. No ties. No commitment. Just two people— a man and a woman—enjoying each other for as long as their time together lasted. That was all this interlude with Adam could be. It was all she could allow it to be.

"All right. He's forgotten." She forced herself to meet his narrow stare with a level look of her own. "I'll see you later." Kara felt as if the forced smile was about to freeze on her face.

"Later," Adam agreed gruffly, allowing her to turn and leave the cottage.

As he watched her walk away down the beach, Adam considered hanging up on the commissioner and following her, but prudence won out and he reluctantly decided not to give in to the tempting impulse.

Besides, Adam reminded himself, he and Kara had an agreement. No strings. No ties. It was without a doubt a practical, sensible rule. And he was nothing if not a practical, sensible man. Ignoring the little flicker of doubt in the back of his mind, Adam returned his attention to the obviously harried man on the other end of the line.

UNABLE TO KEEP HER MIND on her work, Kara paced the bleached oak flooring of her cottage, determined not to think of Adam. But that proved impossible; her rebellious eyes kept drifting toward the sparkling curve of coral sand, watching for him. Waiting for him.

"This is ridiculous," she muttered, glaring out over the turquoise water. "You can't possibly love the man; his world is light-years away from yours."

He was also not interested in commitment or permanency, she reminded herself firmly. He'd told her that from the beginning. To expect a future where none existed was sheer folly. And that, Kara realized, was the crux of her problem.

Faintly annoyed with herself, she sat down at her rattan desk and selected an almanac from her stack of research texts. She did not believe for a moment that Adam was over at Colin's house, fretting foolishly about their relationship. No, he was undoubtedly deeply immersed in the reason for the commissioner's telephone call, his attention focused solely on his own future. His own ambitions. Determined to do likewise, Kara began to read.

"That must be some dynamite book."

As Adam's deep voice broke her concentration, Kara lifted her head, surprised to see him standing over her.

"I didn't hear you come in."

"I knocked, but your mind was obviously somewhere else."

"Arizona."

"Arizona?"

"It's illegal to hunt camels in the state of Arizona," she explained.

Adam smiled. "I'll keep that in mind the next time I visit Phoenix."

Kara nodded. "I certainly hope you will. After all, it wouldn't do for the police chief of one of the neighboring state's largest cities to be arrested for camel poaching."

"The commissioner would probably hit the roof," Adam agreed easily as he pulled up a chair.

"And wouldn't that be a disaster," she muttered.

His brow furrowed in response to her acid tone. "Are we fighting?"

"No."

He continued to study her thoughtfully. "Good. Because I don't want to waste time fighting, Kara. Not with you. Not now." He took her hand in his.

"What did his lordship want this time?" she asked, struggling to keep her voice steady as he brushed his thumb lightly over her knuckles. How was it that such an innocent touch could make her feel as if her bones were melting?

"I can think of better things to do than to talk about the commissioner," he murmured, lifting her hand from his.

Adam's self-assured tone, the practiced gesture, the gleam in his deep blue eyes, all these things reminded Kara that theirs was a relationship based exclusively on mutual pleasure.

She gave him a very sweet, very false smile. "You're not answering my question, Adam."

He ran his palm up her arm. "We can talk about him later," he insisted.

"We'll talk about him now."

Muttering an oath, Adam forced his mind off the satiny texture of Kara's skin and back to their conversation. He didn't want to waste time talking. But despite his need to make love to Kara, Adam realized that by ignoring her repeated request, he would be giving her the idea that the only thing he wanted—or needed—from her was sex.

And though their love life was admittedly enjoyable, Adam had the vague, uneasy feeling that something else was happening. Something that he vowed to think about the first chance he got.

"Martin Henderson, the current police chief, had a heart attack early this morning."

Kara drew in her breath. "Is he—"

"He's going to be all right," Adam assured her quickly. "But it forces his retirement a few weeks early. At the moment, San Francisco is without a chief of police at the same time the union is threatening to go on strike. That's the reason for the commissioner's call. *Now* can we make love?"

Kara was surprised by what appeared to be desperation in Adam's tone. "In a bit of a hurry, aren't you?"

He ran his hand down her hair in what was meant to be a soothing, apologetic gesture. "I don't have any choice. My plane leaves in less than two hours."

Kara had been expecting this since the moment she had entered Colin's kitchen and seen Adam's grim face. She had spent the past hour preparing herself for Adam's departure. The news came as no real surprise: why did she feel so rotten? She forced back the stinging tears behind her eyelids, vowing that she would not cry. She would not ruin what had been an idyllic holiday by behaving like a clinging, hysterical female.

Annoyance was the safest emotion Kara was experiencing at that moment. Allowing it to surface, she struggled to keep her voice steady. "Gee, Adam, don't let me hold you up."

Adam was seized by a sudden urge to cross the room, lock the door and settle things between them once and for all. This relationship was not going as he had planned, and he had never been one to allow himself to lose control of any situation. Unfortunately that damned agreement they had made precluded such behavior.

"No," he said harshly. The wicker creaked in protest as he rose abruptly from the chair. "I'm not going to fight with you, Kara. Not today. Not now." He caught hold of her upper arms, yanking her to her feet. Before she could utter a word of protest, he had flung her over his shoulder and was striding into her bedroom.

"Adam," Kara insisted, "I don't want to do this."

"The hell you don't," he muttered, tossing her onto the bed.

His masculine arrogance made her temper rise. "Don't you dare tell me how I feel!" she shouted. She was on her knees, her hands on her hips. "I know you, Adam Lassiter; you'd never force a woman . . . What are you doing?"

He yanked the polo shirt over his head. "Getting undressed." His belt dropped to the floor. "You're wasting valuable time here, Kara."

"Put that shirt back on."

"Kara, Kara," Adam said on a deep sigh, "you're making things extremely difficult." He trailed his hand over her shoulder, pushing the strap of her white eyelet camisole down over her arm.

"I'll tell you how you feel," he said in a low, deep voice. "Soft. And warm. And inviting." His eyes held her unwillingly captive in their stormy depths. "I don't think I'll ever get enough of you, Kara, no matter how long we're together."

His intense look, lush voice and tender touch conspired against Kara's earlier resolve. She felt her body warming with a raw, primitive passion that should have become familiar by now, but hadn't.

"What would the citizens of San Francisco say if they found out that their new police chief had this bad habit of tossing women around?"

"Probably ruin me," he said easily, satisfied as he felt Kara relaxing under his stroking hand.

She linked her hands around his neck. "We wouldn't want to ruin you. Not when this promotion is the most important thing in your life."

Adam's expression turned suddenly sober. "I wonder," he murmured, more to himself than to Kara. Before she could react to that unexpected change of tone, he ran the back of his hand down her cheek.

"I am going to miss you."

Kara tried to speak, but the sudden lump in her throat blocked the words. She swallowed. Thrusting her hands into his hair, she pulled his head down.

"You're wasting time," she complained as she pressed her mouth desperately against his.

He was hers, Kara thought wildly. For this golden moment Adam Lassiter was all hers. She didn't have to share him with the commissioner or the city council. They could forget about the police union, the press and all the residents of San Francisco who had their own claim on Adam. Kara refused to consider them just as she refused to think about tomorrow. There was only this glorious, shimmering moment.

Adam had known many women, but as Kara covered his flaming flesh with openmouthed kisses, the havoc she created in his body became increasingly uncontrollable and he realized that Colin had been right. All the women he had known before had come from the same mold. Sleek and sophisticated, they had fitted easily, comfortably into the world he had created for himself. Predictable. That single word had defined his entire world these past years. Until now. Until Kara.

His hands were not as gentle as usual as he stripped her clothes away, but Kara did not want tenderness. Distantly, she heard the sound of tearing and welcomed it, wanting nothing more than to feel the heat of his naked flesh against hers.

Their bodies pressed, their limbs entwined as their passion crested. Adam felt Kara's fingernails digging into his shoulders; her body trembled as his mouth swept over her skin; he heard her soft moan of surrender as he eased her thighs apart. He took her then, with a wild driving need that made her cry out with pleasure as she arched her hips to meet him.

Together they spiraled out of control as urgency and passion reigned. The past faded, the future was nothing but a dim blur. There was only now. Only this one perfect moment. That was all either of them could allow.

"I'D NEVER CONSIDERED MYSELF to be a selfish man," he murmured later. They had dressed and were sitting on her lanai. "Until I met you." He drew his fingers down her face, leaving a trail of glowing heat. "I want you to come with me, Kara."

Kara struggled to read the real message in Adam's suddenly shuttered blue eyes. What was he asking of her? "To San Francisco? Why?"

"I don't like the idea of being away from you," he said. His calm tone concealed the fact that a giant hand seemed to be squeezing his gut in two. "I thought you might be feeling the same way."

Kara felt as if she were treading on eggshells and didn't particularly care for the sensation. She had always been the frankest one in the family—with the admitted exception of

Maggie—but ever since meeting Adam, Kara had found herself censoring not only her words, but also her thoughts.

"Oh, Adam," she said regretfully.

Adam frowned, wondering why Kara seemed so hesitant. Had he misread what they'd shared? Had those blissful hours meant so much more to him than they had to her? Adam didn't think so. He decided that for some inexplicable reason, Kara was still afraid to commit herself. And as much as he wanted to demand that she stay with him at least long enough to watch their grandchildren feeding frozen peas to Moby Dick's progeny, he warned himself against pushing her.

He toyed with the ends of her hair. "You'd like San Francisco."

"I always have," she agreed. "How long would I have to be away?"

"I was hoping you'd want to move in with me. Indefinitely."

During Kara's long silence, Adam found himself growing increasingly frustrated by his inability to keep this affair on a steady keel. He was accustomed to controlling his relationship with women: invariably he set the pace and they followed; he established rules and they obeyed.

His last lover had laughingly accused him of being a benevolent dictator when it came to the opposite sex. When he had denied the charge, she had assured him that it wasn't an insult. All women, she had claimed, whether they would admit it or not, secretly wanted the man to be in charge. Adam had found that idea highly reasonable and eminently practical.

The problem with Kara was that he never knew from one minute to the next what she wanted from him. What she thought of him. How she felt about their relationship.

"I don't think that would be a very good idea, Adam. What would people say?"

"It wouldn't be any of their business."

"Of course it would be," she insisted. "Your entire life would be their business, Adam. Look how many times the commissioner has called you just since you got down here. When you're supposed to be on vacation," she added pointedly.

Because she'd been the one who'd talked him into tracking down Brett Britton during what was supposed to be his vacation, Adam thought that to be the most ridiculous statement she'd ever made. But knowing that he was walking on very thin ice, he struggled to remain calm.

"Are you saying you're jealous of the commissioner?"

Her eyes widened in disbelief. "You can't really think that."

Of course not, he admitted inwardly. But he only shrugged. "What am I to think? You haven't exactly been open with your feelings."

"Me?" She flung her hand against his chest. "I've always been an open book," she declared not entirely accurately. "It's you who keeps pretending to be someone you're not."

He narrowed his eyes. "Are you telling me that you don't think I'm capable of being chief of police?"

Kara was not fooled by his casual tone—not when his eyes gleamed with that dangerous light. "I think you'll make a dandy chief," she snapped. "Of course you'll have to buy cases of those antacids you were popping steadily when you first arrived here, but the raise in pay should cover the increased medical bills."

"I was under a lot of stress," he declared defensively. "That's what this vacation was all about."

"I know that. I also know the stress will be worse once you get back to the city. And I refuse to sit by and watch you work yourself into an early grave, Adam."

As his frustration grew, Adam took her by the shoulders, tempted to shake her. "It'll be rough in the beginning," he admitted. "But things will eventually calm down."

"Will they?" she asked quietly.

His fingers tightened. "Okay, so maybe they won't. But the pressure-cooker atmosphere comes with the territory, Kara. It's a package deal."

She was trembling as she tried to work up the nerve to ask the question. "If it's so terrible, why do you want the job at all?"

Stunned, he dropped his hands, rose from the wicker chair and began pacing in long strides back and forth across the small deck. "Because it's what I want," he insisted. "It's what I've always wanted."

"Will it make you happy?"

Her words put him on the defensive by recalling the conversation he'd had the night of the luau with Michael Tiernan. He spun around, glaring at her across the bleached oak flooring. "Dammit, I'm not your father!"

She put her hands behind her back so Adam couldn't see her twisting her fingers together. "I didn't think you were."

"But you're comparing me with him."

"That's ridiculous," she threw back. "I was only comparing your situations. My father was a highly respected surgeon, an important man—"

"Who didn't exactly chuck it all to live out a Gauguin fantasy, Kara," Adam retorted. He knew he was handling this badly, but seemed unable to help himself. "He didn't stop being a doctor, dammit!"

"And there's no need for you to stop being a policeman," she insisted. "Just why do you have to be chief?"

How could she not understand? "For us!" he shouted. "I've wanted it for me, yes. But lately I've wanted it for you, too. For us."

Kara could only stare at him. "But I don't want you to be a police chief, Adam. Oh, I might feel differently if I thought it would really make you happy. But I don't believe it will," she insisted defiantly.

"I suppose you'd be contented living with a mere cop?"

Kara wondered what was behind his acid tone. "Of course. If he loved me, I'd also be happy living with a beachcomber. As long as he was a happy beachcomber."

Adam still couldn't quite believe her. "You're a woman."

"Congratulations, you've noticed," she said with mock sweetness.

Kara didn't like the way this conversation was going, either, but she and Adam were like two runaway trains on a downhill grade. Things were getting more dangerous by the minute, but neither seemed capable of putting on the brakes.

He'd begun pacing again. "Women want their men to be successful," he insisted.

She shook her head furiously. "I don't know about all those other women in your life, Adam Lassiter, but this woman wants her man to be happy."

He laughed, but the sound held no humor. "That's what you all say. Then, once you get married, all you do is gripe about what a loser you're stuck with."

If he had struck her, Kara could not have been more stunned by Adam's bitter statement. She swallowed. "If that's what your wife did, I'm truly sorry, Adam. But you're describing her. Not me."

He turned around and fixed her with a furious, disbelieving stare. "How can you possibly understand?" he demanded. "When you live down here in lotusland, talking to fish and collecting seashells?"

That stung. Kara rubbed her throbbing temple with trembling fingertips. "I certainly understand how it is to be driven, Adam," she said quietly. "Believe it or not, I used to be a workaholic myself."

"You're kidding." He would have been no more surprised if Kara had suddenly told him that she was a Soviet spy.

She took a deep breath, wanting her voice to be strong. "No, I'm not. Six years ago, I was making quite a name for myself in television. I was writing, producing, creating new shows."

Her laugh was as flat as her voice. "Believe it or not, in my little world I was nearly as important as you are in yours."

Stunned, he sat down on the arm of the chair and took her hand in his. Adam realized he was about to discover why Kara's family was so protective of her. Why her eyes had become shuttered with pain at unexpected moments. And why she had clung so tightly to the magic of the islands.

"What happened?"

She forced a grim smile. "I started out a lot like you, popping antacids and aspirin around the clock. I was working eighteen to twenty hours a day, and when I'd finally fall into bed, my mind would keep turning over all the things I thought I should have finished that day. I wasn't sleeping, I wasn't eating, and pretty soon I began to have some pretty weird phobias."

His fingers curled more tightly around her ice-cold hand. "Such as?" he prompted softly.

Remembering, she was amazed that she had been such a basket case. It was as if all that had happened to some other woman. Some other Kara Tiernan.

"It'll all sound foolish."

"Not to me. Nothing you could do could be foolish."

"I became afraid to drive on the freeways," she confessed.

Adam, who had been expecting some dire, fatal confession, stared down at her. "Is that all?"

Kara wondered what had made her think he might understand. "It became an all-consuming phobia," she insisted. "My hands got sweaty every time I got in a car, my ears rang, I couldn't breathe. It was like having an anxiety attack. I think I began blacking out.

"In fact, I know it," she said firmly. "That's the only explanation for the accident."

"Accident?"

"I ran my car off an exit ramp at an interchange and landed upside down on the northbound lane of the San Diego freeway. I was coming home from the studio about three in the morning, and because I was practically alone on that stretch of the road, the police figured it must have been a suicide attempt."

Her gray eyes, as they looked up at Adam, begged him to believe her. "It wasn't."

He lifted her hand to his lips. "I believe you," he said simply. "How badly were you hurt?"

"I spent some time in the hospital—a broken leg, a few fractured ribs, minor things like that. When I got out, I came back to Kauai. I've been happier here than I ever imagined I could be."

"Did you ever think that you could be happy back on the mainland?"

She shook her head. "I belong here on Kauai."

Not for the first time, Adam damned the Tiernan stubbornness that flowed in Kara's veins. "You're hiding from reality here," he insisted. "It was only a phobia, Kara, not a fatal disease. Phobias can be cured."

"I know that. But I like the person I've become the past five years, Adam. I thought you did, too."

"Of course I do, but you can be that person in San Francisco just as well," he insisted, almost shouting.

Kara had been considering that from the beginning. From the day she had first started falling in love with a man from the mainland. She shook her head decisively.

"No, I couldn't. If I moved there, I couldn't just sit around waiting all evening for you to come home. I'd try to keep up with you the same way I used to try to keep up with my family.

"Pretty soon, I'd be back in my old routine, and you'd be spending all your time trying to soothe the commissioner and wheedle money out of the city council for the police department, and there we'd be, two workaholics who'd be lucky if they saw each other for five minutes a week."

She was close to tears. "We'd destroy everything we have together, Adam. And that would break my heart." Her eyes filled and she forced herself to look out over the sparkling turquoise water.

"But you're tossing it away by not coming with me," he argued.

She rubbed away the free-falling tears with her knuckles. "I don't have any choice."

"We're going to have to talk about this some more," he insisted. "You can't just drop all this on me out of the blue when I have a plane to catch."

"There's nothing left to say."

Adam wanted to stay there, to hold her, to make love to her until she gave up the ridiculous idea of throwing away a love that was as rare as it was beautiful. But he couldn't think of anything he could say that would change her mind.

He reached out and cupped her downcast chin in his hand, lifting her tear-stained face to his. "We're not finished yet, Kara, not by a long shot," he promised gruffly.

As his mouth covered hers for a long, intoxicating kiss, a treacherous sob escaped her lips. Whirling away, she ran into the house, tears streaming down her cheeks.

As he turned away and began walking down the beach, Adam felt his own eyes grow suspiciously moist.

12

TWO NIGHTS LATER, Adam sat in the dark, nursing a tall glass of Scotch. The high-rise building was in the center of the city; the scene from every window was spectacular. As the purple shadows of dusk gave way to night, the moon created mysterious shadows in the mist that hung over the icy waters of the bay.

The city lights were wrapped in a soft blanket of fog that dulled their brightness, and down on the darkened streets, the car lights looked like fallen stars. A few blocks away, the Transamerica Pyramid thrust into the dark fog-shrouded sky. The magnificent view had never failed to lift his spirits. That night was an exception.

He'd gotten what he wanted. What he'd spent almost every hour of the past years working toward. He was chief. The mist-draped city perched atop the more than forty hills beneath the window was his. So why did he feel so rotten? The answer was simple: Kara wasn't there to share it with him.

Before the appointment had been announced that afternoon, he had had lunch with a furious Colin Tiernan. Over thick steak sandwiches, Colin had accused him of being at best a damned fool. Or at worst, a bastard. Adam readily agreed on both counts.

"So go to her," Colin had insisted.

"And lose my job? I'm not the kind of man to let my wife support me."

Colin had muttered a pungent oath that Adam, in years of police work, had never heard. "So you get a damned job on Kauai," he said. "What's so hard about that?"

"Doing what? Polishing seashells?"

Colin had tossed back his head and polished off his beer. "You're supposed to be an intelligent man," he growled as he got up from the table. "You figure something out." With that, he had marched out of the restaurant.

So now, Adam thought grimly, *I've not only lost the woman I love, but my best friend, as well.* He was wondering what else could go wrong when the intercom buzzed.

"What is it, John?" he asked the doorman wearily, expecting an emissary from the commissioner's office. As it was, the commissioner had not bothered to hide his annoyance when Adam had turned down his invitation to a celebratory dinner which would, of course, have included the press.

"A Mrs. Langley," the disembodied voice offered.

Marilyn. Just what he needed. Adam wondered when the plague and pestilence would arrive.

"Send her up," he said resignedly.

"Adam," Marilyn gushed a few minutes later, brushing by him to enter the room, "you have no idea how excited I was when I heard the news. I just had to take a chance on catching you at home." She smiled, with a brilliant flash of teeth that reminded Adam exactly how much all that bridgework had cost him.

"Well, here I am. Want a drink?"

"Scotch would be divine. With a splash of water." She shrugged out of the mink coat, tossing it casually over the arm of a chair before draping herself seductively on the sofa.

He mixed her drink, refilling his own glass at the same time. Adam had a feeling it was going to be a very long night.

"You're looking well, Marilyn," he said as he handed her the glass.

That much, at least, was the truth. She was as slender as ever, her firm body showcased by a black silk dress with a plunging neckline. Diamonds twinkled at her wrist, her throat, and her earlobes, and her hair was a soft shade of blond that Adam knew could only be natural, or achieved by regular visits to a very expensive beauty salon. Since Marilyn had been a brunette when he had married her, Adam was grateful he didn't have to pay her hairdresser's bills.

She gave him another of those seductive smiles as she crossed her long legs. "Thank you, Adam. You're looking quite well yourself." She glanced around the room. "And I have to admit, I'm surprised by your apartment. It's very tastefully done."

Adam's eyes circled the room, as well, seeing it as if for the first time. A professional interior designer he had once dated had decorated the room in shades of gray, ranging from the soft silver of the walls to the deep pewter shade of the lush carpeting. Tasteful graphics hung on the pale gray walls, illuminated by track lighting along the high ceiling.

The furniture was contemporary—molded, modular pieces covered in a gray-and-black striped fabric, combined with a lot of black lacquer. A collection of small sculptures were displayed on chrome-and-glass shelves. The mood of the apartment was every bit as controlled, as reserved, as the man Adam had been pretending so hard to be all those years.

"A slight improvement on the Salvation Army rejects I had when we were married, right?" he asked dryly.

"Well, our apartment was a little tacky."

Bright green eyes that eight years ago had been a nice soft hazel gleamed as she observed him over the rim of her glass.

Contact lenses, Adam realized. So he hadn't been the only one who'd set about turning himself into another person. Marilyn was a revelation.

"Good heavens, Adam," she protested as she nearly choked on her drink, "perhaps you've upgraded your taste in furniture, but don't tell me that you're still drinking this horrible cheap Scotch?"

"I like it," he answered amiably.

"That's the same thing you always used to say when we were married," she accused. "I never believed you."

"You should have. I never lied to you, Marilyn." There was a brief silence between them. "Speaking of marriage," Adam said at length, "how's your husband? Darrell, was it?"

Her lashes fluttered as she lowered her eyes. "Dennis," she corrected softly. "I'm afraid he and I are separated."

The warning bells that had begun tolling in the back of his brain now pealed resoundingly. "I see."

Marilyn blithely waved away the thought of her cardealer husband with a flick of her diamond-encircled wrist. "Let's not talk about me," she suggested. "Not when it's so much more exciting to talk about you."

Rising in a smooth, lithe movement, she gave him a look that could have been poured over a waffle. "How thrilling that you've achieved what you always wanted."

They were only inches apart. Adam caught her wrist as she was about to touch his face. "You mean what you always wanted," he corrected quietly, returning her hand to her side.

A familiar fury flashed behind the emerald-green contacts for a brief moment. Adam had to admire her control as she forced her lips into an attractive little pout. Eight years ago she would have slapped him for less than that.

"I'll admit I wanted the best for you, Adam," she said silkily. "But I was only thinking of you. It was always you."

She wet her lips in a contrived manner that almost made him laugh. "I've followed your career all these years, Adam. As hard as I tried, I could never get you out of my mind."

"Then you should be thrilled to hear my news. Since you're so interested in my welfare."

She put her hand on his arm. "I've already told you how thrilled I am," she reminded him.

"Not that news."

Her eyes narrowed suspiciously. "Whatever are you talking about?"

"I mailed my letter of resignation an hour ago."

"You're joking," she insisted. "It's a trick to pay me back for leaving you for Dennis."

"It's not a trick," he corrected quietly. "And as for you leaving me for that Chevrolet dealer, Marilyn, I should have thanked you for that years ago. It was one of the best things anyone has ever done for me."

"You bastard!"

He wasn't surprised when she tossed the Scotch in his face. What the hell, Adam figured resignedly, it only showed that people never really changed, no matter how they altered the packaging. Wasn't that what Kara had been trying to tell him all along about himself?

"I think it's time for you to leave," he said calmly.

"Past time." Marilyn scooped up the mink, draping it around her shoulders in a haughty gesture. "I should have known better than to have expected you to have become a gentleman."

"You should have known," he agreed with remarkable cheerfulness. "Oh, and Marilyn?"

"What is it now?" she snapped, turning in the doorway.

"I wouldn't worry about catching another husband. There are a lot of Mercedes dealers in the city; perhaps you can trade up."

With a curse, Marilyn Langley slammed the door. Adam went into his boring gray bedroom and began to pack.

KARA WAS AWARE OF HIM the moment he entered the room. First there was the slight squeak of the screen door being opened, then the soft shush of her bedroom door, followed by his soft footsteps as he made his way toward the bed. All these sounds drifting into her subconscious mind as she slept told Kara that Adam had returned.

But it was something far more elemental, emanating from the very essence of the man that roused her to instant awareness. She sat up, pushing her tumbled hair out of her eyes.

"I'm so glad you're back," she whispered.

The mattress sagged as he sat on the edge of the bed. "You don't sound very surprised," he said, his lips caressing her scented hair.

Kara traced his face with her fingertips, as if to reassure herself that this was not a dream. "I wished for you. And here you are."

Nuzzling against the soft fragrant cloud of her hair, Adam nodded. "And here I am."

He drew her into his arms, running his hands up and down her back. The satin of her sleep shirt was cool against his palms, but Adam knew that her skin would be warm.

He kissed her then because they had been much too long apart. Although by the calendar it had been less than three days since he had been with Kara, since he had held her in his arms, Adam felt as if it had been a lifetime ago.

"You didn't lock your door."

"This is Kauai, remember?"

"How could I forget. I've come to a decision," he said, fighting to remain calm while his stomach went on a roller coaster ride.

His lips, as they lingered at her throat, were more intoxicating than champagne. Her blood hummed under their touch.

"A decision?" Kara asked, enraptured.

Unable to resist touching her, Adam drew his hand over her breast, feeling a tightening in his loins when Kara pressed herself instinctively against his touch with all the feline grace of a sleek cat. He had promised himself all the way to Kauai that he was going to do this correctly. That he was going to savor the moment, giving them both something to remember for the rest of their lives.

As she slowly trailed a fingernail up his thigh, Adam realized how difficult it was to linger, to savor, when every nerve in his body was screaming for relief.

"Dammit," he said, moving his hands to her shoulders, "I can't think when you're driving me crazy." He reached out and turned on the bedside lamp, flooding the room with light.

Kara had been about to suggest that he not think at all when she stopped to stare up at him. "I don't believe it," she whispered as a glimmer of hope made her dizzy.

"What?" Adam demanded, feeling unreasonably nervous. He followed her gaze to his vivid aloha shirt. "Oh, this. I bought it at the airport when I got in."

His casual white cotton slacks were rumpled from all those hours on the plane, his eyes were bleary and red-rimmed from lack of sleep and he needed a shave. Kara thought he looked wonderful.

"It looks very good on you," she said.

"Think so?" Adam had felt a little foolish buying the red-and-orange flowered shirt, but the attractive young

Eurasian saleswoman had assured him he looked just like a true *kamaaina*. "I have to admit it's comfortable."

"You look very sexy," Kara assured him. "Even better than Tom Selleck; you'll have to fight the women off with a stick."

"I only want you, Kara." His expression suddenly became sober as he handed her a small box tied with gold cord. "I brought you a present."

"I absolutely adore presents," she said with a warm smile that reminded Adam of a tropical sunrise.

"It isn't emeralds," he apologized uneasily. "Or diamonds, or French perfume or any of the expensive things you deserve."

"Adam—"

"But," he said gruffly, "it reminded me of you."

His rough, serious tone almost proved her undoing. With fingers that trembled slightly, Kara slipped the gilt cord from the white box. She lifted the lid, giving a small sigh of pleasure at the piece of stained glass that nestled on a bed of white tissue paper.

"Oh, Adam, it's lovely. Thank you." She lifted the rainbow suncatcher up to the light. Her walls, her ceiling, the floor, were all suddenly covered with rainbows.

"There's a card."

So there was. Kara was nervous as she plucked the small card from the tissue. "There's a lifetime of rainbows out there," Adam had written in his bold, precise hand. "Let's wish on them together."

"Oh, Adam."

His stomach was twisted into knots as he took both her hands in his. "I know we had an agreement," he began seriously.

"Adam—"

He immediately cut her off with an impatient wave of his hand. "An agreement that made a great deal of sense at the time. You were happy living in Kauai; you had your family, your work, your snorkeling. Horatio. Moby Dick.

"I was fighting off a case of professional burnout before returning to a job I'd been working toward for years. Neither of us had the time or the inclination to get involved. It would have been highly impractical."

"Highly," Kara agreed quietly.

"Well, I don't care about practicalities any longer. I don't give a damn about what's sensible and what isn't, what's prudent or not. I know I swore I wasn't looking for a wife, but that was before I met you. Before I knew how good things could be between us. So I'm revoking that agreement here and now."

Frustrated by the clumsy way he was handling this, Adam had to stop. Nervously, he began pacing the room.

"I've been thinking about what you said. You're right, I wasn't very happy as a captain and I would have been miserable as chief. I became a cop to help people, to try to make a difference. Not to spend all my time playing political football."

"When did you come to that conclusion?" she asked.

He lifted shoulders in a weary shrug. "I don't know exactly. I suppose tracking down Britton had something to do with it; I'd been in a supervisory position for so long that I'd forgotten how much I liked to get out on the streets."

His expression was grim, unyielding. "I've resigned, Kara. And I've come to Kauai because I need you."

Kara examined her nails. "Are you by any chance asking me to marry you, Adam?"

Adam stared at her. "Of course I am."

"Oh."

This wasn't going at all the way he'd planned. "Damn."

"Now that's romantic."

"I forgot the most important part."

Seeing the distress on Adam's face, Kara took pity on him. Rising from the bed, she kissed him with all the fervor of a woman in love. When she finally tilted her head back, her eyes were sparkling.

"I'm listening."

Adam took a deep breath. "I love you, Kara."

Joy, pure and bright, bubbled through her. "How handy. Since I love you, too."

He ran the back of his hand down her cheek. "I don't want to give up police work," he warned.

"We have policemen on Kauai, too, Adam," she reminded him.

"I know. You're looking at one of them."

Her eyes were bright with hope. "You wouldn't tease me about something as important as this, would you?"

"Of course I wouldn't. Chief Kanualu hired me on one condition."

Kara arched a copper brow. "What's the condition?"

"That I don't try to take his job away from him." He smiled at the memory of his brief but highly satisfying conversation with the island police chief. "I assured him that I have absolutely no desire to be anything but a plain old ordinary street cop. Or beach cop, whatever the case may be."

"Good heavens, you're certainly not plain, Adam," she said, unbuttoning the flowered aloha shirt. "And you could never be ordinary."

The shirt landed on a chair across the room. "As for being a street cop—"

"Yes?"

She whisked his belt from its loops. "How fortunate for you that I've always been a sucker for men in uniform."

"Then you'll marry me?"

"Since my entire family would disown me if I didn't," she said, "I think I'll let you talk me into it."

Her smile was dazzling, rivaling the brilliant radiance of the Hawaiian sun as it pierced the early morning sky with shafts of purest gold.

Kara held out her arms. "*Aloha nui*, Adam. Welcome home."

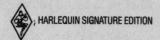

JUST ONE NIGHT

Hawk Sinclair—Texas millionaire and owner of the exclusive Sinclair hotels, determined to protect his son's inheritance. Leonie Spencer—desperate to protect her sister's happiness.

They were together for just one night.
The night their daughter was conceived.

Blackmail, kidnapping and attempted murder add suspense to passion in this exciting bestseller.

The success story of Carole Mortimer continues with *Just One Night*, a captivating romance from the author of the bestselling novels, *Gypsy* and *Merlyn's Magic*.

★

**Available in March
wherever paperbacks are sold.**

COMING NEXT MONTH

#189 THE PERFECT WOMAN Libby Hall

Kim Troussard wasn't Sean Stevenson's type—
and vice versa. But they were repeatedly drawn
to the same place at the same time . . . like
magnets. Proving, in spite of themselves, that
opposites *do* attract.

#190 FAMILY MATTERS Carla Neggers

When Sage Killibrew got an urgent request to
meet her long-lost grandfather—and bring him
$40,000 in a briefcase—she couldn't say no.
Which is how she ended up entangled with a
sexy, very *un*grandfatherly rogue named
Jackson Kirk. . . .

#191 FULL BLOOM Jayne Ann Krentz

Emily Ravenscroft had blossomed! Taking
charge of her own life at last had brought her
into close and thrilling contact with strong-
willed Jacob Stone. But her meddlesome family
was determined to break their bond. . . .

#192 THE FLIP SIDE Vicki Lewis Thompson

When Amy needed a friend, Jack was there.
Then deep affection began to turn to ardent
desire . . . for both of them. Was she ready to
risk a friend to find a lover?

Take 4 best-selling love stories FREE
Plus get a FREE surprise gift!

*Coming Soon
from Harlequin . . .*

GIFTS FROM THE HEART

**Watch for it
in February**